ANONYMA

A Novella by Farah Rose Smith

New Orleans, Louisiana

© 2019 FRS

© 2022 Grimscribe Press

Cover art and design by Donna Dean

All rights reserved. No part of this publication may be reproduced, distributed, or transmitted in any form or by any means, including photocopying, recording, or other electronic or mechanical methods, without the prior written permission of the publisher, except in the case of brief quotations embodied in critical reviews and certain other noncommercial uses permitted by copyright law.

Published by
Grimscribe Press
New Orleans, LA
USA

grimscribepress.com

CONTENTS

Prologue	1
Chapter One	3
Chapter Two	13
Chapter Three	19
Chapter Four	25
Chapter Five	29
Chapter Six	35
Chapter Seven	39
Chapter Eight	43
Chapter Nine	47
Chapter Ten	51
Chapter Eleven	55
Chapter Twelve	59
Chapter Thirteen	63
Chapter Fourteen	75
Chapter Fifteen	81
Chapter Sixteen	89
Chapter Seventeen	93
Chapter Eighteen	97
Chapter Nineteen	101
Chapter Twenty	105
Epilogue	109
About the Author	111

TRIGGER WARNING

Domestic violence and sexual assault.

PROLOGUE

I T WAS A cult, and I was a part of it.

But I am, and have always been, myself.

Men write songs about girls like me, and then they kill them. I still think of him that way—his songs were ice-in-photographs. I should have been the girl who lived in the way of everything, jumping around corners and speaking *far too* loudly—to awaken, to rise. A girl made woman in a cage.

It's her bath time. The yellowed envelope sits on my desk, unopened for over a decade. Picking it up with a delicate tilt, an old print slides into my hand. A stone grows in my stomach, lurching back and forth as I glance to the bottom right corner of the picture. *NB*, scraped in gold. And on the back in faded ink—*Anonyma*.

The great I-AM.

CHAPTER ONE

Nicholas Georg Bezalel sits in his office chair—a throne of sorts—peculiar in height, with cushions upholstered in black velvet and sharp metal spires—pure onyx, he clarifies—rocketing out towards the ceiling. Formidable would be an understatement. Being in the building alone is an exercise in artistic endurance, far outpacing the cognitive dance of a day at any museum in the city. Bezalel is pleased to hear this, as it is a direct validation of his design manifesto.

"*Modern † Gothic* starts with a feeling," Bezalel says. "To describe those initial emotions with words would make no sense logically, in the grand scheme of allowing you in on the process. The act of creation, of production, of endurance. These are all my secrets, you see. What I can say is that the style has permanence. It is art, but more importantly, *Modern † Gothic* is a way of life."

Bezalel has been working on this building, nicknamed *The Noctuary*, for twenty years. A 190-floor work of wonder, it's his most elaborate architectural construction to date, three times the height of his famed 2013 construction in Sedona, *Babel*. We asked him about the origins of that project. "A domed chamber of voices, an installation, that is all. That is in the past. Let us speak of the now!" He laughs when asked if he is aware that the media still calls him the *Echo-man*.

"Of course."

From the time Bezalel began the original sketches of *The Noctuary* in '91 until its completion (still ongoing), Bezalel says that he was (and is) the subject of a peculiar dark fanaticism, which he channels into his work. "I saw the building itself in a childhood dream, not long before the death of my parents."

For twenty years, the façade of what was originally the location of the Hegland building caught Bezalel's eye. "I found myself in a state of mourning for it. Like an open wound of mortar. Cracked, crumbling walls and the decay of colors, too-bright and grotesque. Unsightly would have been an understatement. I've always detested the brightness of the modern age. The sentimentality, the robotic warmth of it. But there was something there, to be dissected, if nothing else. A voice of sorts, begging for resurrection. The space alive, striving for breath."

When the owner of the original building, businessman and curator Dalton Hegland, passed away after a sudden illness, Bezalel found himself in the position to purchase the lot.

"It was a dream. One that grew from tragedy, I would add. Dalton was a great man. An advocate for the arts, always present, charitable, lively. We had our differences, but we came from different schools of thought. This happens. And many lively discussions breed from such dissension. This is food for any artist, these disagreements. Though I think even Mr. Hegland would be in awe of what has become of this space."

Bezalel resides on the top three floors of the apartment building, in a sprawling loft that goes above and beyond the decadence of the lower levels.

"It was my opportunity to go a bit mad."

His liberal use of plain crystal and texturized ornament adds dramatic contrast to the stark walls and marble floors. That is a function of the first floor only, he explains. "Sparseness spurs innovation, but one cannot do without entirely." The art collection in the ground floor entry hallway alone deserves an article, ranging in the dark and decadent works from symbolist Belgium to the dark and dreary machinations from the pages of *Modern † Gothic: Sorcery In-Design*. When asked about his feelings after the movement took hold in various other mediums—including literature and fashion—he is modest, but pleased.

"I feel I played a role in invigorating a style that was already deeply-rooted in American culture. Hibernating, perhaps. But certainly living." *Modern † Gothic* could be described to the layman as an updated, polished, and decadent variation of gothic architecture, with interior design aspects that incorporate the aesthetic sensibilities of

Symbolism, Surrealism, the Avant-Garde, and goth subculture. "It started with a dream, as all things do."

In regards to *The Noctuary*, Bezalel began by making all of the walls black. "With master works, there must be consistency and integrity." The dark palette would allow for elaborate furnishings and décor in various modes of decadence, depending on the room. The palette barely strays from black, white, red, and silver.

"Here we are, in New York and somewhere utterly indescribable. That is the gift of *Modern † Gothic*."

A robust man with impeccable style, Bezalel's platinum curls take the shape of a falling tower. His bright green eyes are piercing, though sunken—suggesting that sleep is a rare occurrence for him. A curious figure in a black turtleneck, long leather jacket, and black trousers, he is nonetheless immediately visible in the sea of shadow ornament. Despite his overpowering presence, he is jovial and warm, welcoming us into his office. Along the farthest wall hangs a collection of images archiving his 2000s architectural and interior design works in pictorial form. His assistant—a young, decidedly Victorian-looking ginger woman in all black—carries schematics and sketches in from his enormous archive room. He leads us through a hallway to the projection room to talk through his design process.

"I'm not so vain or idiotic to feign pure originality. But I would hope, as my mentors have said, that enough of my DNA is mixed in there to make it mine." Bezalel cites G.E. Von Aurovitch as his idol. "Von Aurovitch was the godfather of *Modern † Gothic*. Not myself. Without him, there would be nothing. I would not be alive today if it were not for that man. His influence, and his works." Bezalel became accustomed to designing these rich, experimental interiors from his decade-long residency in an area he refers to vaguely as "Northern Germany."

"I can tell you that there was a great deal of study done in Thuringia, in obscurity. An attempt at refining the style before returning to the States." He goes on to tell us details of his apprenticeship that have not yet been told to anyone. "In Thuringia, on the banks of the Unstrut, I embarked on excursions that were tantamount to walking in the steps of Von Aurovitch. A privilege for any artist." He is less forthcoming about his philosophical discoveries during this time. "Those must stay with me, I'm afraid."

Bezalel was born in Berlin in 1972, an orphan. He never found out who his parents where. "Unlike other children in that situation, I felt no intrinsic desire to seek them out. Why go looking for someone who left you?" When Bezalel was nine, he was adopted by a banker and his wife who were visiting from London. "They were kind people, though distant. My adoptive father had an extraordinary library where I was left quite often, to my great delight. I didn't complain." When asked of his adoptive mother, he is more reflective. "There was a sadness in her that I could never quite put a finger on, though I suspect it had to do with her husband's countless affairs. He was a profound man, but an absolute rascal."

After his adoptive parents' tragic deaths in a house fire in 1987, Bezalel used the fortune left behind to emigrate to the United States. He attended New York University, with the dream of becoming an architect. His time there was filled with complexity. He describes an environment that was not so much hostile, but indifferent to his work. "It was a comprehensive education, but comprehensive in its lifelessness. Frank Lloyd Wright idolization gets pretty stale after the first dozen lectures, though I can reflect on his work in kinder terms now." Despite his discontent with the curriculum, he doesn't regret attending school. "It was that discontent, that persistent melancholy, that served as the birthplace for *Modern † Gothic*. I immersed myself in the dark designs of failure, of missed opportunity, and alienation. Swirling in dreams brought on by that very anxiety, I found my purpose."

After graduation, Bezalel was faced with a choice. Return to London and accept the job he was offered at a small architectural firm, accept an even more pitifully-paying job at a firm in New York City, or go to Berlin to retrace his roots. "It wasn't about family or finding myself. Who I was, who I had become, was very clear. It was the sense of existing without refined purpose that haunted me. I felt I could find out more about that purpose in Germany."

He spent a year in Berlin and an additional five traversing the villages and landscapes of Thuringia. "Seeing the places that inspired Von Aurovitch and Friedrich meant a lot to me. I learned to see nature as art during those years." We asked him if he considers himself a Symbolist. He takes several moments before answering.

"To say I started as a Symbolist, there is merit there, I suppose. In fragments. I did a lot of writing while I was out there. I certainly am not opposed to nature. It's power, particularly the unknown power that we cannot ever really see. I immersed myself in that, tried to understand it. There was an energy there I could never quite capture, obviously bigger than myself. That's true horror, isn't it? But that's not what I wanted to explore, or display. You can't create or control the natural. At least that's what I discovered. The decadent power is booming. Art as life. Art as power. Art forging its own reality. I have long-admired the illumination of other worlds in all manner of design. This, of course, is dripping with the lifeblood (or deathblood) of Von Aurovitch. Here, in architecture, in interior design, in natural installations, in fashion, in photography, either directly or indirectly, I was able to mold and maneuver with a specific energy that, in a way, bridged the gap between the Decadent and the Symbolic by getting to the philosophical nerve of coexisting opposites, and honored those I drew from. But I still think it isn't representative of any one movement from the past. It is, quite simply, *Modern † Gothic*. It is its own movement, its own improvement, its own reality."

In late 1999, Bezalel moved to an even smaller flat in Berlin—dirt-poor, but re-invigorated. "I was closest to knowing what I wanted to do with myself at that point, though the discontent still weighed heavily." His apartment was above a small gallery, which proved to be synchronicitous. "The landlord saw some of my sketches and brought them (without my knowledge) down to the 'curator,' his wife. She fell in love with them. She invited me down for tea and asked to see my portfolio, which was nothing but a taped-up notebook at that point." She took a liking to him and offered to exhibit his work, provided he could get presentable works ready in a month. "I survived on sausages and crackers and didn't shut my eyes for weeks. By the time I'd finished, I thought I'd be in the permanent state of a waking-dream forever. I still wonder if that's what is really going on."

Another peculiar act of synchronicity brought good fortune to Bezalel. Though now a disgraced figure in the United States, the then-lauded Dr. Brague Collins, medical researcher and noted art collector was passing through Berlin with his wife Marcella, a notable scholar of Von Aurovitch's works. "They were, obviously, both devoted admirers of Von Aurovitch. I think that's why they were curious to stop by, since I noted him as inspiration in the leaflet I taped up in cafe windows. We ended up having a very nice chat at the opening gala." When asked if they had any further correspondence, Bezalel waves his hand. "Nothing more than trivial encouragements and niceties. And my condolences after the loss of his wife and daughter."

Despite his hesitancy to speak about the matter, it is assumed that this interaction with Collins spurred him on towards a new trajectory which include a return to New York City and the opportunity to show his work at the Neue Galerie in 2003. "That exhibition was the beginning of a monumental shift in my fortune."

By that time, Bezalel had accumulated a body of work consisting of paintings, etchings, drawings, sculptures, and small-scale models of curious structures he had seen in his dreams. "I had enough to go around and pitch things without looking like a *complete* ass, just barely."

Bezalel became recognizable in art circles fairly quickly after the exhibition at the Neue Galerie, prompting a level of excitement from both industry legends and newcomers to the art world. "There was a degree of theatre, there. In the mind, I mean. Sartorially, as well. There wasn't a lot of careful planning, but by then, I had lived a strange enough life to be intriguing to these people." His reputation grew as a mysterious figure, rarely present at events himself, though actively producing new material. He maintained focus on his idol, Goethern Ellis Von Aurovitch, as a source of motivation. "Whenever I'd get exhausted, or discouraged, I'd remember the enormous adversity he faced, and how most of his works were never even finished. Yet he lives as a legend, a sorcerer of literature and the arts. One can only aspire to such heights in modern times."

Bezalel became inordinately famous in the New York City Avant-garde circuit by the time *Babel* was erected in the Arizona desert. In 2016, he attended the Met gala and was introduced to his current fiancé, supermodel Coreya Witciewicz. When asked about their first meeting, Bezalel smiles and clasps his gloved hands together. "Leland Moller had dressed her in one of his outfits based on Alfred Kubin's sketches. When he introduced us, I expected her to know very little about the design. Turns out she was a fan of Kubin, Von Aurovitch, various other fantasists and artists I had known and loved since childhood. She is unlike any woman I have ever met before."

Witciewicz lives with Bezalel in *The Noctuary*. Now retired from the runway, she is at work on her own fashion line, which is said to be deeply rooted in the philosophies of *Modern † Gothic*. When asked if she serves as his muse, he laughs heartily.

"She is my darling. I don't think I ascribe to the practice of having *muses*, per se, as I have found it often to be too exploitative, too direct. Coreya helped me move along the aesthetic into the realm of fashion. In the beginning, perhaps had she been there, there may never have been *Modern † Gothic*. I would have been far too distracted to be productive at all in that arena."

When asked about his infamously macabre and controversial photographic exhibition of 2009, entitled *Anonyma*, he grows more reserved. "That project was an offshoot of a greater idea that never really manifested as I wished it would have. What we made of it, I am still proud of." The exhibit caused a great deal of controversy, spurring criticism from feminist groups. To this, Bezalel merely shakes his head. "There is a point at which one must separate the art and the artist. There is an intrinsic link, of course. But there is less of me in those images than there is of what I was trying to evoke. They misunderstand me" When asked about the process of creating the infamous images, he becomes brusque. "Let us move on."

Despite the intrigue that surrounds him, Bezalel is much more accessible than many would imagine. Most of his works capture the dark designs of what one would assume is a tormented mind. In sharp contrast, Bezalel appears content. Coreya enters the office, looking as though she has just stepped off of the runway. Her chestnut hair is tied in a top-knot, long billowing black fabric displaying her beautiful form in all its noir-pinup glory. She is a woman of duality, both regal and eccentric. This evening, she is bringing Bezalel his letters—written correspondences he maintains with artists, writers, and thinkers around the globe. He smiles, taking the letters and kissing her hand.

When asked if they plan to have children, Bezalel's eyes flare with excitement. Wietciwicz is less enthusiastic, changing the subject. "Nicholas has far too much to work on at the moment, as do I. You know what they say… you can have it all, but not at the same time."

And the work Bezalel has ahead of him is plenty. He has revealed his latest project, an adaptation of Von Aurovitch's obscure fantasy play, *The Curse of Ariette*, which will be performed in *The Noctuary*'s own underground theatre, *Antangelus*. "The play is dear to me," Bezalel explains, his hand migrating to his chest. "I can't say that any project has felt quite as important. I want to get it right." He lets it slip that he intends to play the lead role. When asked if it is a vanity project, he laughs heartily. "Every project is a vanity project."

The Noctuary doesn't seem to fit into that category upon first observation, but with a careful look into Bezalel's literary tastes, one can begin to put together a theory which suggests that he is bringing the objects of fantasy worlds—worlds of his own, and others—into reality.

"*The Noctuary* was a dream construction of my own, but there are elements of existing things in there. The idea of a black tower with a great golden theatre hidden in the underground floors… while I would love to claim that as my own innovation, I have to give credit to F. Krespel von Rehm, who wrote of such a place in the final chapters of *The Almanac of Dust*." When asked if there are any works he still aspires to draw from, he thinks deeply for some time before answering. "As a fan of Von Aurovitch, I have naturally had a fascination with *The Scaerulldythareaum* for some time. However, I have only managed to come across a few of the excerpts he translated shortly before his death. To understand entire chapters... well, that would be beyond my wildest hopes. So much so, I dare not think of it. I do not wish to be depressed!" And depressed he is not, despite the celebration of all things morbid and macabre in his designs. "It is precisely that, a celebration of life amid darkness."

Critics have called Bezalel a sorcerer of design, a maverick, a savant, the "menace of magic," the "*Echo-man*." He rejects all titles, preferring to see himself as a passenger through the world, doing what he can to preserve the fantastical in a society overrun by what he perceives as frivolous banality. We asked him if he plans to return to photography. "I would like to, if the conditions are correct."

Upon request, Bezalel leads us to the next floor, which houses the entirety of the *Anonyma* exhibition. He is characteristically quiet, as one would see him at a gala or museum. Our producer points to the most infamous image of the nameless model—unconscious, wrapped in gold wire, suspended over a green lagoon. Her face, as it is in all of the photographs, is obscured. We ask him about the impact of the series—if the controversy gave him pause about the depths he is willing to go in the creative process. He reflects on Von Aurovitch again. "If you have seen the archived images of *The Blue Lady*, the portrait he painted of his wife, you may come to understand risk, and all that it entails in art." Before we can ask him to clarify this confusing answer, Coreya appears in the doorway, noting that he has a meeting in twenty minutes. We are ushered out without further comment on the series.

The observation most people make about *Modern † Gothic* is that it has led them to find a balance between cognitive richness and materialistic extravagance. Bezalel acknowledges how the traumas of his youth led him to a new and comprehensive philosophy that nurtured this concept. "The instability, the darkness was unpleasant, but the only constant in my life. In it I began to find comfort, familiarity. The inverse of the uncanny. I wanted other people to understand that they could make peace with their demons. Find solace in the unfamiliar. Work with the darkness." Now a celebrity figure, Bezalel reflects often upon his years of struggle. "Success doesn't cast a veil over the years I spent ostracized in this city. The absolute outcast. To reject those roots would be a full rejection of myself."

Pick up any magazine, and you can see the enormous impact that Bezalel has had on modern culture. The styles and tastes that once alienated individuals have now been embraced by the mainstream. While New York City is no Silver City, it has rather the transported energy of the Middle European avant-garde, a phantasmagoric shadow kingdom curated by that sorcerer of design, Nicholas Bezalel.

CHAPTER TWO

I HAVE THE LOOK of death again, underneath the icy hue—spectral light on a lifeless stage. Sorcery and dark wishes are never without a conjurer. They set their roots deep beneath the hardwood here. All the stage, a sinner's web—and I, the captured fly.

I find myself in a passion of dying, more so than in previous days of early waking. I do not want to die, in the strictest sense. Though I am tempted by the dark pull. The passionate embrace of nothingness beyond the wall of twisted life and death. I can think of no better solution for myself in such a state. I fail because my body has withered to the point of atrophy, in a tragic misalignment of age and acuity that can only be attributed to the illnesses festering inside of me. I have been too honest. So honest, that even the mask of glamour cannot hide my deteriorating mind. It is a humiliation unlike any other, to feel yourself on the precipice of death and not be able to censor the cascade of disgrace. I walk in a rickety gambol as of late and fail to stay awake in the acceptable hours. I wish I could see a glory beyond the horizon for me, but it takes only the form of a plunging of the self into the limitless deep. I have no name, though it grows and grows. I feel a phantom weight glide into my chest, as strongly as his heat.

I am Anonyma. A ruin in this city, swept up by blackened rain. I cradle oblivion in my arms; am at war with clocks over lifetimes broken apart in silent stories. I am not without a kind of freedom—the freedom of suffering. But what is to be said of a woman who holds such depths of darkness within her? I am one of these, at best, and never without sight or sound to measure. Walking dead above the ground for years, after dismissal from the clouds, left sour. A bitter hall of whispers, thick with the milk of memories. I bury myself with a daily kiss to scepters and bones. You have found me—bound, and quite alone—warring with the world falling around me.

The girls are laughing and shitting, spitting and giggling. My head is on the stall door, cold with the beating of footsteps. Long black locks dangle in front of my face, escaping the cover of my hijab. I watch—a pendulum of strands sweeping in silence, mourning again—until the girls are gone from me, from here, from everywhere. The lights are dim and set a green cast over the fading tiles.

The cold glaze ripples over the surface of the stage, casting twinkle-twinkles on the tatters of my skirt. The tiresome glow shoots up to the face of every dancer—but not my face. Even the aging beauties have a dignified grace made for acceptance. It shines through their idle attempts to hide their frailty, booking them entry even through the most labyrinthine of doors.

The theatre is a glittering mass of unnatural decay. Upturned noses and the rolling of eyes suit most of the young dancers. They despise the age of it—the garish ornamental embellishments on every wall—particularly the scraping of paint from sculpted faces. Smirks and sneers and giggles. Smirks and sneers and giggles. Smirks and sneers and...

Social ritual. The ritual of battery by the batting of eyelashes. This is the war of women in the slipstreams of worth. Their lithe forms glide across the stage, one by one, exerting all efforts to impress the judges. I make my own crude attempt, so unlike my former self, in form.

The three men watch from the seats, bored and scribbling haphazard remarks on their ledgers, rarely deviating from a delicate "yes" or harshly jotted "NO."

"All right, make a line in the center."

The dancers line up. The bodies are indistinguishable from one another, all having worn white by some strange act of fate. All, save for this body.

Only men in heat pick this body.

"Kim, Sarah, Leah, Keri, Rachel. Everyone else, thank you for your time."

Here comes an accident of anxiety. A chosen dancer standing to my left, with skin like buttermilk and bright blue eyes, turns—extending no effort to conceal her contempt.

"He didn't call you, gimp bitch."

The girls have gone from the bathroom. I can stand at the mirror now. In all the grotesque glory of an ogre, one hundred-fold. I remove my hijab, imagine beetles in my hair and rot under my chin. The decay of my insides working their way out. A father's full lips and a mother's square jaw. Bug neck, deer limb, dark-haired devil. Is this the mark of womanhood? Seeing slime in the face of flowers? This thick mop of black curls, turned to stone? Will I ever hide this mess of broken dreams?

Even in that deep melancholy, one need not feel eternally alone. I touch my tongue to the mirror, unsure of the weight of days bruising either shoulder to the eyes of unseen things. I want to be better—to soar, beyond the confines of this suffering, to a lighter place. Not of death. Death was an act. The act of returning to the endless ever after. I saw it one day, in my reflection beneath the bridge. Cold waters mewed up like a frozen sculpture, scraping the border of this world and the next. Half-blind by cruelty, I stared at the water—the subtle shimmering, ringing bells heard only by a precious, calming aether. On quiet nights in bed, when the tears stain my cheeks and the ticking clock measures my earthly atrophy, I can feel it. A subtle pulse in the air from the land of other. A place of doors wide open—welcoming, warm.

There is something to be said for the stillness of a woman in exile. The faint sway of yearning and yielding. The quiet mess—with feeling, without feeling. There may be some hidden value in the depths of depressive seclusion, but as of now, I do not know them. Can't know them, perhaps. Not with the fright of memory. Burned into my mind, are the images of those days. There is clarity there, so unwelcome that I feel it burrowing into my bones. Some days I can barely bring myself to stand, let alone walk, and attend to all that must be attended to.

I once thought of myself as a great bird, crying over a tousled nest, mourning the sudden loss of the dream of life. Now I imagine myself a rat. A toad, even. Unwelcome in most places. Prodded in others. Always a novelty or abhorrence to those who walk without feeling. There are so many of those. Wind walkers, Walk-and-talkers, walk-and-whistlers, whiners.

The air is black. What I breathe into my lungs barely quenches the need of those sacred elements. My mind conjures an unknown world where fire has taken the place of air, and liquid lungs take in the embers, fueling the cruel organics of some living mass. I think of the elements not yet known—inconceivable to human senses. Too dumb to conceive of them in full, or negate them equally, there is a wishfulness there. That there are things that can be known without premise, without promise. Without the preconceptions of man and earth. I long for the leisure of broken worlds, lost underneath the wheel of the cosmic order.

These are the sidewalks of phantom wanderers. Ugly mules with no other place to roam at night. I count myself among these ghosts. Cars fly—screeching vessels of light and noise—more jarring than they were in the early evening. Eyes on the ground. Hands hidden. Defeat, Defeat. My blanket of death-in-life.

The railing is the first sign of the bridge. I can see the faint glint of it from here. Fast walking comes naturally when resolution tempts the eye. Here is the bridge again. I remember this somber resolve. If I close my eyes, the wind will whip up my hair and I will feel the weight of hands, teasing every strand. In this exodus of mine, this gripping of the cold rail, this feeling of terminal bliss, I am the monster married to the endless night.

I know these waters. I've seen them before. Glared at them in the after-hours, wondering of the worlds thriving beneath the surface. I've closed my eyes and sent my soul out, gliding over the surface of all things, searching for a kind of rebirth. Nature afforded me no such luxury, but the fantasy has lived on days like this. So I return to the bridge again, in airs of torment calling me down down. Into the black water.

Von Aurovitch had a sculpture named *Black Water*. The only piece of this I would come to hate.

Where is that ring? That ringing? That constant ringing coming from? My eyes jerk open. I reach into my bag.

Vava.

My great-grandmother does not speak. She breathes heavily into the phone. We have the bond that only blood-bound women have. She has aged into the arms of nonsense. Tonight will not be my night of departure. She needs me to come home.

CHAPTER THREE

I ENVISION HIM as vividly as when he last stood before me, a wisp of black and blonde approaching from a farther wood. Nicholas Bezalel, the Jester King, the Mastermind of the Majestic. I don't think I've ever seen such a creature—and a creature he was. A Nordic-looking man with long legs like a spider. He towered over all of us, in body, in spirit, in wealth. But something was unsavory about him, and all of us questioned the origin of this phantom.

By chance, or perhaps eagerness, I come upon his image in the city. I *see* the sign, the marquee. I *see* that *it is* him. His face painted a ghoulish-hue ripped from the era of theatrical grandeur. A lion of lace and crystals, plumes of woven ivory fabric circling his head like a mane, adornments dripping down his jester-king attire, a staff of pure light in his hand. This is Nicholas Bezalel, though not quite as I remembered him.

A haunt of electricity tunnels through my senses, bringing back the vision of his face. My eyes shut, tightly squeezing, unable to take the flood of emotions, of pain, that accompanies the memory. I sway in the street, illuminated only by the milk-light of the half-crescent, thinking too much.

The poster hangs proudly, moonstruck and ominous, on the outside of *The Noctuary*. Unable to conduct myself with grace, I stumble backwards, streams of cold air gliding past my nostrils, an enchanting freeze on the precipice of everything and nothing. I thought I had walked on a different street. I thought I would have avoided such a thing.

What might one do, when they realize how many moments were *stolen* moments, placed in the hands of a monster? Am I in the place of regret, or ready to throw up my hands? If all could have been avoided, my mind begins. But it couldn't have been. The little girls lost in a sea of becoming find their nets and crevices. There will be stings and stains, pain and powerlessness. One cannot shield the young from such plays of the soul. It takes its course with each of us. What might I know in truth, if I learn from hearing alone? If I do not live a life on this earth as painful, as erratic, and as real as those before me? Exits presented themselves in rags and riches. Means of escape in the prick of cold metal, or the depths of the river. I could have taken them. I could have. But I didn't. And in that, there is everything—or nothing.

The first time he hits me, I am freezing. Surreptitiously elsewhere—the cellar, the vegetable garden, the home of my great-grandmother, soaked with the scent of basil and pepper biscuits. His anger is unexplainable. I bristle and pivot on my heel, making a quiet maneuver for the open door. I almost make it before a sharp tug of my hair send me back onto the tile. Love is not this much of a mystery.

He tells me that he needs me, and I remind myself of a root in long-winter. Still there, still waiting. A memory in mind of a cyclic bloom. This is nature, isn't it?

I collect silent spells and exist as myself in the darkness. He bursts into a line of ecstatic laughter, almost bringing back the original days. I am more vigilant, and less, all at once. I preserve consciousness in vainglorious self-neglect and recall the tale of the abominable fish and the golden hook. My features return to their normal shape, and I almost remember myself.

It was a day like this. Gentle snow—dense, light—floating down from the aether, blanketing our shoulders and eyelashes. From the distance, Nicholas approached. His steps tired from the agonizing fatigue he'd subjected himself to after the failed ritual. His anger had given way to his pitiful, exhaustive depression. That one element we shared in earnest.

The bridge, barely noticeable in the somber clearing, creaked under the weight of him as he approached. He said nothing. Only stared at me with unreserved detachment. I love this man who means to warp my soul to ash. Who lies and cheats. Who stole my life from me. My joys and my passions, forever tainted by the blackness of his saliva—the rot of his cold tongue. I love this man before me on a stage of blue, in snow—as I see him in a dream, without feeling. I remember him as he was.

All around me I can see the nothing. I have met it, embraced it, allowed it within every orifice, pore, and hole. There is a loathing for the shape of me. I won't look at it anymore. I want to feel his hands on my chest—on my throat. I want to die in his arms as I am. This is love they bottle in a broken world.

There was enough of conversation to hide the void—inattention—that remained in me as constant as the rustling of the papers against the window. *Untranslated*, I think, with regret. I stopped reading long ago, unable to extend my concentration on text beyond the point of form. To decipher, one must understand something beyond the confines of materiality. The essence of writing, from that time—a majestic, dignified gloom, teeth-deep in the workings of a parallel world. Carrying out such a task casually would be a cruel injustice. To carry it out in vanity, as Nicholas had done, would be an affront to nature and the unnatural, alike. He wanted me to translate the book. He wanted to know how the ritual must be done.

While once these dark texts birthed a colored wonderment, now I descend, in stale boredom over them. As discontented as vegetables drowning in slime.

The book itself is a dead man's cologne—fragrant with the thickness of plastic and a faint hint of rot and flowers. I tuck myself in with this finery. Run the cool cover over my thighs and begin again.

Vava is as sick as one can ever be, but not as sick as mother, in her tomb. Home is a house of somber weight. Tired feet creek past the doorway and into the shabby kitchen. Peeling yellow paint and discount furniture, cramped into the most inhospitable of places. She steps around loose plastic bags on the floor, noting it needs to be swept, and leans into the parlor. There sits Vava, in a daze of memory. Hearing me come in, she remains as still as a corpse.

I enter my bedroom, the heat of exhaustion rippling through my legs. After placing my bag against the closet door, I toss one shoe and then the other, glitter heel crossing past dim lamplight and scratching the posterior wall. I don't lie down on the bed but kneel, staring at myself in the mirror opposite me. Sliding off of the sheets, stepping with weighted grace to the chest of drawers beneath the mirror... The lowest drawer pulses with the animal magnetics of bitter memory. I hesitate, sliding the door open, drawing back letters and papers without care, concentration centered on the lowest of contents.

I've taken to an unbridled fascination with the eccentric and untoward early in life, but there was no fascination so entrenched as the one I had for Von Aurovitch. It began with a small clipping in the local newspaper, detailing the anniversary of an exhibition held in the city one hundred years prior.

We basked in the archaic pessimism of Von Aurovitch's works. In addition to his massive catalogue of sculptures, paintings, etchings, and machines, he released two written works. One, a collection of essays from his earlier years, detailing his philosophical leanings and journey of self-discovery in extreme locations across the globe. The other, his fragmented translation of the *Scaearulldytheraeum*, a book purported to have been pulled from a parallel dimension, detailing the most precious details regarding life, death, and worlds beyond the realm of human sight. These were the obsessions that drove him mad, warping his once whimsical and somber art into machinations of madness.

As time went on, and his madness devoured the last of his reason, his creations grew more grotesque, more abhorrent, and somehow, more realistic.

I'm awake—somewhere in the fourth hour, before light, to read. I feel like a ball of filth, but must make something of the morning, despite this. I read the end chapter only and became distracted enough by the pounding in my skull to abandon it. A waste of a day, perhaps? I will take to reading later, provided my condition improves. I cannot take the darkness of these characters now.

CHAPTER FOUR

I AM TRYING TO escape the memories for as long as possible. I hope to finish the ninth Canto of the *Scaearulldytheraeum* for analysis, though progression is slow. The untranslated sections grow more common, the deeper one gets into the tome. I believe it will take me until Spring, possibly even until summer to finish. I would dearly like a draft by Christmas day. That would be the ultimate gift, wouldn't it?

Every year I promised myself love in time for winter. In time to stand together on the woodland bridge, in snowfall. To share one gentle kiss. Another year arrives, without a hope in hell of this. Will it ever manifest? This dream of passion? I don't believe so, though I ask the universe anyway.

All I want in this life is love and independence. A family of my own. I would throw away all other pursuits for these.

It was heard about town that I had my books. Before the dark shadow crept over me, I could often be seen in small bookshops in the northern corner. Those very places that housed aging editions of the most insidious handiwork in the realm of sorcery and daggers. But never fiction. Never fiction.

I tire of myself in every aspect. Life, mind, and cage. I want only to soar beyond this place, these memories. To know love, safety, pride. Worth, even.

It seems so little to ask of the universe, until I realize that the ever-constructing universe is indefinable, and within the body. My body is tired, tired, broken by him him him. Though today improved profoundly with the passage of hours. A dark storm brews on the horizon. I sat outside, enjoying the heavy sting of wind on my cheeks. I took a walk afterwards, through the woods on my usual path. I was taunted by memories for a bit, but quickly disengaged from my conscious mind. A moth, floating gently to its demise, shook my past from me.

I miss him so much sometimes. Is this possible? Or maybe the sense that I meant something, even if that something was dark. This sensation, this aching, will pass with time, won't it? For now, I will sleep, I will read, I will study life literature, and I will heal alone.

It would seem that within every book I read that examines the *Scaearulldytheraeum*, there are deeply disparaging excerpts aimed at women. I can't help but feel hurt, or angry, every time I encounter such a passage. They speak of the shame of womanhood. Of the weakness and evil of femininity. I will never understand such an attitude. Understand the origins, the precursors of its development? Of course. But to think one can't reason beyond such a dark set of interpretations...

I have never felt more like a woman. In the love I feel for a man who breaks me open, the despair I feel over those who have sought to destroy me, all for being both woman and the possessor of a deep, prevailing resolve.

There are giants who hold books from the motherland, chronicling the events of the first earth. They have no patience for the whispers of small men. Hazy plots of grandeur soak his conscience. I have heard these words—doom design—in the book. No resentment lingered as heavily as the great resentment: that anything given in love, freely, would never be returned. Not honestly.

Oscilla, my pet snake—a blind, white beast as tired as myself—lurks on the far bookshelf. She watches me turn the pages, in angst.

It is unlikely in such places that the use of truth is wholly effective. Distancing myself from alchemy and the wisdom of sages, it became clear to me that curiosity, when justified, will never have a proper audience.

I am afraid to reveal myself as ready, hiding instead in the black thistle of my dreams. I awake to the sound of breaking glass. Shards glittered across the bed sheets, damp from the remnants of the shattered bottle. A broken rhythm crowds my senses. Everything I had ever heard buzzed in my ears. Heathen whispers from the monstrous corner of the universe.

It's long past midnight. I'm in bed, staring at my breasts, guilty and at a loss as to how they have become so large. They are beautiful, yes. Though I think, rather wasted. I could be a great lover and a greater mother.

CHAPTER FIVE

HOUSED IN THE netherworld of *The Noctuary* tower, the Majestic theatre is a hovel of confabulated circuitry. A wishing-well of edifice and smites. The shows housed there are brusque and demented, always with glimpses of savage body parts under lights of red and blue. Dirt, blood, water, spew, and dust. These were the holy markings of the Majestic stage, and no matter who came in and tried to gussy up the dump, these elements would remain. But there is no dust that sparkles quite as eerily as that which sits atop peeling gold.

Twenty actresses had played Ariette in twelve cities across the East coast. All were unknown actresses, or so I am told. They were not even billed by their true names. I've heard whispers that they were street girls that Bezalel had picked up on his night haunts, but I think not. I was not of his traveling troupe and cannot claim to have been witness to any motivation or materialization of malice. There is no such information in my eyes, ears, mouth, and these hands are worthless with the ink dwellers. I know nothing of Bezalel before this city. But of all that happened here, I can tell.

I loved the play. He knew this. Knows this. Of course he would bring it to my city, where I couldn't resist attending. *The Curse of Ariette* was the masterwork of another Von Aurovitch accolade. One who has been dead almost a century. Goethern's blue lady, the centerpiece of the whole affair, drives the plot, the myth, the legend. She was the only one Von Aurovitch ever loved. All else fell into the bounds of rancor and contempt. How she had ascended these ranks to find sanctuary in his dark heart had remained a mystery to all—and a fascination.

I remember the place, and it brings me to my knees. How he came to replicate a place that could scarcely be rediscovered in the woods is beyond the capacity of my mind to fathom. He must have returned to the bridge long after the last of our encounters. He must have studied it with particular obsession. How else could he have resurrected it here, on the stage? Without lifting a hand of his own, conveying only thoughts and ruminations to those in charge of construction?

The outline of trees can be seen in the far distance. They are starkly black, backlit by dark blue light. Tree branches loom overhead, swaying slightly. A little girl appears. She has dark hair and piercing eyes. The little girl wanders, seemingly lost and in awe of her surroundings as the dark shadow of a human figure looms in the background, watching her.

The girl stops, noticing the moving shadow. She remains still as the shadow grows. A masked man appears, walking slowly towards her.

The girl remains still as the man looms over her. The mask he wears is both majestic and frightening, an amalgamation of theatrical purity and whimsical predilection.

Bezalel moves his thick hair back to show his long, pointed ears. The little girl is startled. As she stares, Bezalel reaches behind his head and slowly unties his mask. He removes it delicately, revealing his strong, painted face. Despite the profound makeup and contouring, what bleeds through is the face of a man decaying far before his time.

The actor reaches his ghostly hand over his face and slowly removes the mask. He lowers it, revealing a profoundly structured, and faintly wicked, face. His cheekbones look to be cut from marble. His eyes are extraordinarily light, even for blue. The man is a decaying masterpiece. But this is not the thought on his mind as he lowers the mask. His eyes are on... me.

Why have I come here?

He would never be seen without the sleekest of attire. His black jackets were buttoned up to the neck at all times. The silver buttons were engraved with indiscernible occult symbols from whatever ancient tome he adhered to. He wore velvet spats over his leather shoes, adding an old school flare to his gothic countenance. But it was hardly done in the manner of kitsch and camp. Bezalel was a force of profound elegance and class, and it hid the dark fire well for a time.

Nicholas Bezalel was, for certain, what one would call a put-together man, but this was not without its drawbacks.

He appears to be a mere haunted shadow of his former self, although there is some forbidden strength in his demeanor.

The little girl struggles to stand up. She stumbles, crying as she adjusts to her newfound blindness. When she finds her footing, she quickens her pace, leaving the realm of the elves and exiting offstage.

As she runs away, four figures emerge from the distance. Elves wearing masks. One in the center approaches Bezalel and removes his mask. He is an emaciated, strange-looking man. Bezalel turns to him.

I sit in quiet contemplation, watching the scene.

Bezalel shifts several steps as a jagged icicle descends from the heights of the trees and impales the girl. Blood splatters all over the stage and into the air. It looks so *real*.

I am awake within the memory of our first encounter. An exhibition of the works of Von Aurovitch. I stood in silent study, enraptured by one of Von Aurovitch's earliest paintings, *The Mare of A Thousand Wounds*.

He had the common light—a slight twinkle in the eye. They project the devil outside, guided by the manipulations of Bezalel. But I know nature, as I know myself, and the devils inside live as freely as those who deign to erase them.

He has no recrimination against himself. Behind the curtain of specialty, his scholarship and her artistic grandeur, behind the façade, the element of decay rolls on.

"Anonyma. My blue lady."

That pleasurable pulse deep within the flesh came again. Something in the upstanding tower of platinum curls atop his head. The thin lips, the icy eyes. There was a hint of abnormality whispered only through ocular glints, askew in the most subtle of tendencies. But of gravitation, there was never any question. A hint of psychopathy lingered in the woman who chose that man. Or perhaps masochism, to the most archaic degree. My pallor, that of poltergeists, reflected in his overcast spectacles.

He stares at me in that old way, and I feel the closeness of my grave. Is it death that I love and seek without rest? Is this why I have come back to this place?

I wonder about the need for this union. About the cries I stifle inside of me. I was weak, always. Quiet-tempered, hesitant, and true. This is no failing, of woman or man, or anyone. In a neutral world, such things become transient hues in a kaleidoscope of personalities on the living surface. In danger, however—conflict, passion, war—they become a liability.

There are those who will seek to blame me for my burden. Who see the bruises on my face and believe I deserve them. They have to believe that. How else could they reconcile such a thing, before them? If I were innocent, and marked, then an injustice has been done. An injustice has been laid out before them. And one is meant to act in the face of injustice, not walk away. Cowardice lives in that walking. So, they believe that I am deserving of this mark. Of this horrid life of mine. To think it could happen to them or their innocent children. That this is the way of evil. And you turn from it every day, not wanting any involvement. What one fails to realize is that this, too, is left up to the cosmic rest. I have no hatred for them. No more than I do for myself.

I walk to the offices in the back of the theatre. It looks like the waiting room of a doctor's office, but with a desk and fewer chairs. The lights are fluorescent, and the walls are white. Nicholas is in the doorway. He is no longer in his theatrical garb and wig but wears a thinly-cut black suit. His hair is short and blonde. Without the makeup, his features are obvious, but so is his exhaustion. A haunted man.

He says my name. He pulls my body to him, and I am as limp as the first time.

We collapse together in this mess. He holds me around the waist, sliding his head down to rest on my stomach as I lean against the door. His face turns away, but I know what lies within him now. Those thoughts that stir with proximity to the body of your bearer—the one who robbed you of him all those years ago.

I can feel the wetness drip from eye to mouth, and then to me. In this way, I know I am not forgiven. How could one expect any less from such a man? He wields and he wanders with the darkness of untold worlds, never without plans. My stomach turns beneath him. There will be little room for denial this time. There is something in him, beyond the confines of broken love and undying rest.

This depression carries none of the subliminal delicacies of the romantic tradition. There is, rather, a sharp brutality to my melancholy. The kind of somber weight that causes a dull ache in the chest and rib cage, a slowing of motor skills, and the sense that a black veil had been cast down upon me from some unknown region in space-time. There will be no enjoyment in former passions, no rationality even in the simplest of conflicts. My mind had become a battleground, riddled with the pounding and scraping and wheezing of a hard-fought and never-ending war. One of thoughts, one of emotions, and one of memories.

CHAPTER SIX

PALE ROSE RIBBONS cascade from my wrists. It is the darkest third of night—an endless whir, beyond sleep. In this house, I toss and turn in fear of death. Cold materials, Soaked in wax and the light of dreams, fearing only what is coming from the vastness of the night. In this house, three bellies press to the wall of dust—His. Mine. A phantom of another, fading life.

My child dies within me. I remember the horror as though it has already passed. With a river of depression flooding through, transfixed by the menacing angles of the room. He is at attention in a fury of movement. An orgy of bones and rats sweeps across the floor. All circles around what he says in silent language. It is past bliss that haunts the womb so brutally.

I pour the urn, the milk of moons, into the fire, tendrils of blue flame reaching up towards my hair. There is an air of doom-festivity. Blue walls, black curtains, the gaze of expectation—of loss—in every eye. Black jelly slides off of the dinner plates, our feast one of starvation and decay. As intimately horrid as the meal of mirth and mouse. My passion for him is painful, endless. I twist my hips, lifting the skirt away from this living porcelain. Out of the half-smoke, still high from the heaviness of dreams, he pants and pulls at the ribbons, approaching from behind. He has touched the dark mist again, the look in his eye belonging to some second self, amiss in the green mist of mischief.

Closed eyes scream into the celestial stillness. First dress, then panties, then bra, are ripped off and thrown onto the floor. Cold lips press against my back. He sits in his chair, pressing his body against mine, cock growing hard against my legs. Fingers glide across my breasts, my stomach—mouth sucking at a nipple as three fingers penetrate this hall of life. I cry out, silver passion pouring down my thighs. Collapsing into his arms—black fibers of cloth rubbing up against my skin—he carries me to the couch. The frost in his heart pours out—white dust falling over my body.

Loving him is a large, senseless feeling. I fall in this deep-pink passion, swelling breasts at the suddenness, the violence. At once I would flee and succumb to this advance. There is love and hate in it. Struggling against the quiet nausea of submission, weighed down by the immensity of him, he slides me forward against the upholstery, twisting me on my stomach.

Those who build a world of objects can only love like this. He removes his black clothes with startling swiftness. I await this disaster of intimacy. Penetration, and the ache of a hideous heart. He yanks my hair back, disheveled, a sweeping pendulum of strands. The madness opens up in him. His cock is hard as stone. He shoves himself inside of me, his pale prisoner, holding me down in ecstasy.

The black celestial hue resumes its lividity.

He is rocked back by a vision of clouds traversing the cosmos. Cocks and roaches and kings of old worlds, arms lifted in oppression of pleasure, lips of death pressed against their hearts. Awakening from this vision, transfixed by my gash, he hears me choke out, "The gash in me is as the eye in heaven."

Sickness seeps into me, awake in the multiplicity of love. Vulvic magic turns and pulls him back, a scorpion coach down ice cold halls. A finger to the face, with venom gloves in the mouth and then the slit. They are the slaves of dreams and greying shrouds. Voiceless vermin chew at their toes. A mouth appears and closes in the darkness. Laughter echoes off of the empty plates. I never wanted to be part of this dark magic.

His fever is strangled by the festive night. He holds my soul against my own desire, drinks from the holy gash, as red as madness—a sea of concentration in womb-glass. He continues his gothic recess, tongue writhing in and out of me. He pours the blessed milk of moons over my breasts, dreaming of fetal wonderment, petals, ash, and oak. My skin glows blue and then white, womb water bursting forth from her netherworld. He takes some in his mouth. Worms leave the milk through unviolent effort.

"I am a mortal on a slab," he whispers, lacking the will to know the magic night. I await the birth of a mother mist. Thirsty wings, devoid of light, beat in the corner. A mountain's glowing fire glows from the nearby window. Moon rays fall on my breasts. The crystals on the sill corrode and burst, amethystine shrapnel lodging into them.

There the motions grow, man to woman, letting dismay wash over a broken womb. *Cradle not his madness in that den of life.* I no longer want to know love in ashes, guiding the improbable with a gray worm mind—aloof and afoot in the muted crawl with no part to play in this mud—no dreams of clenching or regret.

A thousand eyes and mouths sing out, an explosion in Dionysian space, sound covering us with the weight of an opaline shroud. I whisper, through the pain.

"The gash in me is as the eye in heaven."

I fill myself with the lightness I once knew while dancing. A blossoming, frothy feeling in the hands and legs. It will not be long before I am mangled, unfinished. Before he breaks my body with magic. He twists my head around, running his tongue across my teeth and down my throat. I feel some dark design crest in his energy. Folds of black cloth curl betwixt cunt and sadness. The night is luminous. Moths swarm against the window. I watch them in a haze of hunger. He can almost feel another time against his chest. Another name on his lips. This I have known forever. Holding back his own stream of horror—of tears—he reaches around, holding my breasts, riding harder.

The silhouette of time stands by the door. He cums inside of me, his voice a burnt husk of memory, crying out from his lost internal wilderness. Pausing a moment, he pulls out, pressing his head against my back.

"I love you," he says quietly.

I know he is not speaking to me.

CHAPTER SEVEN

I GET THAT sense under false light. That I am as unnatural to them as the ceiling yellow is to the stars. An invention—no—an abomination of men, forged in-hand for uses guiding them toward their own impatient stardom.

He bought the dress for me. The perfume, the necklace. All his tastes. I speak no opposition. They are beautiful. More so than I feel worthy to wear. I think rather that these items wear me, and I am no more than a warm hanger.

He rages. I can never know why. Pacing back and forth, he begins to let out his usual exasperated sighs. This is before so many things. The time before my education, so I speak. I ask him what is wrong.

Nicholas remains quiet, pacing from the camera to the midway place in front of me. Continuing to check in the viewfinder, he clearly isn't satisfied with what he sees. I shift uncomfortably.

"Don't move."

"I thought maybe if I put my arm here?"

"Be quiet."

He stands, with one hand on his hip, scraping at the loop of his belt. He approaches me, looming over—his shadow cast over my head and chest. He closes his fist and delivers one hard punch to my face.

The force is enough to drive me into shock, but not enough for me to black out. The pain—the pain is beyond comprehension. I lift my hands to cradle my nose, but he shoves them back in place. Blood gushes from my mouth, where I bit down on my tongue.

"Stay where I have you."

This is the strongest I have ever felt fear inside of me. I struggle to contain the guttural shaking brought on by the assault. Nicholas stands behind the camera, peering into the viewfinder. The tell-tale clicks commence, and I am staring into space, speckled by aura. I will not move but fly over this mess. It is the first time I fly outside of myself to escape the pain.

Nicholas says he needs me in this way. That I have some unspoken thing in me, reflecting in the unlit pool of time. I know better—know that there is nothing so brilliant in me that could pull the shadows out from unknown places. Not to sing, or laugh, or dream. No—I am, in this agony, without magic of my own. But I raise up a little thing in me that lives as purest magic.

I am Anonyma. A falsehood through a lens.
Washing in ashes, choking on the fumes.
Posing with dead bodies, defiled by rotting fingers.
Thorned wires cutting into my naked skin.
My legs beaten dead with hammers, with hands.

The cult. The cult. They are a cult of madness. I try to avoid the fetid dwellings of his acolytes by the twisted morass on the outskirts of the city, no matter how often he insisted that she make nice with them. Coreya is more intelligent, more corrupt. More knowledgeable in the lore and twisted ethics of the book, able to quote sections at length and uphold herself in every exchange.

Coreya wants me with her in the evening. She means to walk under the moon in hatred, cursing several victims with their names. I am not afforded my own, and yet this is what she asks of me. To accompany her in this dismal affair. I have had enough of quiet despairing as I paste on smiles. Enough of false compassion for these—sickly and inbred.

Coreya is a freckled ghost. Always hopping and skipping and cutting toes from toads, and other such natural horrors. I would not say I hate the girl, had I a decade of distance to remove her from the here and now.

I envy women of that kind. Are they in on the torment or merely too stupid to know what is being done to them? How can they see themselves as willing participants when all evidence points to the contrary? And yet, here I am. A willing participant, but without joy. Without the free spirit of the inimitable cool, outspoken girls around me. I am not one of these.

This is where Nicholas Bezalel fails in his imitation. And it is that—imitation of higher art—a higher man. Von Aurovitch was no man of pomp and circumstance. He had no harem of devotees. None that he would allow within his realm of living. It is true that he had his admirers. Mostly among the intellectuals in the art community. Those obscure few who saw the depths before madness took hold and left him to his hermetic decrepitude. Not even historians know where his end occurred.

Nicholas wants to be a hero. He wants this dark princehood in art and magic. He will not have it. This, I know. Because one without magic shows his hand. In this case, exposing his throat. We are in a war of languages unknown, and he is losing at a faster pace than even his brilliant mind can recognize. He thinks himself a man of absorption, but he has no stomach for this kind of learning. There are those things that remain unreachable to the eyes and minds of men.

I tell him I love him, and the heart blood pours through the soul's umbilical. Up into the aether, blackest blackest blood. When it spouts, I hope they will not think less of me. I hope they will understand love, and this love, without disappointment.

He has in him all the self-aggrandizement and obsession of the worst of accolades. This he hides masterfully, beneath a façade of reason. Or logic. Artifice, in its most loathsome form. He sets himself above all others, save for Von Aurovitch. Fancies himself the prodigal son. This will be his folly, and his finality. It betrays all that Von Aurovitch believed. I am no true fan, he says. For I cannot name every brush stroke, every sculpted mass, every creature! I cannot recite the passages in the adapted tongue. I cannot even hypothesize as to the inner thoughts of the blue lady. This, I tell him, so that I can let my ribs heal from the last. I know her through her eyes, even without the original to examine. The blue lady, her pain, her suffering—might Von Aurovitch have been such a horrid man as this? Or was her pain something deeper? Something of her own lifeblood, her own making? I will never know. One can only know themselves, and even this takes a degree of sorcery.

There is little to be said of love in a feeble body. It is a repulsive, pulsating heap of disgrace and shame in the human sphere. Expectations? How might I have them, if they do not lead to a shadow, to a grave? They are lowered so quickly in an afflicted youth. The black cloud of dreams shields the golden possibility—that life, in all its glory, is possible to all, regardless of condition. But is this true? I think so. Though one will struggle, struggle to the end to see the clearing. The eternal blockage—doubt—will lead the feeble-bodied astray. Because it is all we have here in the human sphere. All we know. That life, as it should be, is a foreign luxury, unavailable to us because we cannot reach, we cannot breathe as the others. In this, we are the other. With only a dream that other worlds linger in the dark distance, calling us home.

He penetrates me from behind, and I remember why I stayed. There was not a drop of magic in the world so potent as his touch. No matter the mass of evil in it, the persuasion, or the looming agony.

He smashes the book into my head. I fall into the vase, shattering it and myself over the marble. A single shard leaps up in eccentricity, lodging itself daintily above his stomach. He pulls it out. The telephone rings. I stare, breathing and blinking and breathing and blinking, as he walks over and picks up the receiver. With the eerie calm, he asks who is calling.

"It's your father," he says, holding the receiver down to me. My father is dead. He laughs and hangs up the phone. I lift my bleeding arm from the floor. As I open my mouth speak, Nicholas wipes the blood away with his kerchief. Every touch turns my stomach black.

At the root of all things was love, despite the difficulty. Our most valued moments were those of a sitting silence. Merely being together in that most basic state of togetherness. No words, no worry. Only presence and acceptance. I hope, in that moment, that such a thing is possible with my daughter. But this is the dream of agony that stirs up after dread-soaked dawns and memory play.

CHAPTER EIGHT

I SEE MYSELF as darkness in the lightest eyes, and this is the trick of the gray soul—to blind the innocent. But was I innocent? Seeking out such majestic, elevated company? Not in the same way as Coreya, or the others. Not to be cradled and launched into artful prestige. Only to love and be loved. In this way, perhaps I was more selfish than even they.

His incantations brought applause. I thought nothing of it until returning home. A small child cradles a dead kitten, screaming of the "bad noise" from the woods. Repulsion, shame become my waking realities. The smells, the sounds, the emotions—always descending to the great black morasses I have yet to escape.

I fail. I see myself from the outside in. This is why I fail. I wake up, thick with milk.

He wants to tear the heavens from my eyes. The crown from my soul. I have not even come to know these things within myself as I should have.

Do I hate him? I will have to think on it. No—I don't believe so. I have made little room for hatred in the soul corrections of age. I cannot even piece together his face in my mind. I see nothing but an odious blur of white and yellow, hovering where his form and features used to be.

I could awaken within myself, a living woman. Awaken, and walk out the door right in front of me. I shatter mankind over myself like blue beads.

Breathing in black smoke was never a desire of mine, but I make note of the creeping urges that return, like so many bugs out from the subterranean mist.

My cheeks are sunken in now—deep, deep. Jaundiced, anguished, delirious from the noise. I imagine blood as powder, contemplating the movement of ruin in a flash of red dust. He knows how I abhor the primordial slime. Where eyes are masks, not mirrors, and the dead things creep unto the light to sip-sip-sip it to oblivion. These are the halls in which I am left behind.

I escape to the palace of no-man, where they bow to me. Spectral walls close in on all, but not without caution. The vivid body, disemboweled as a majestic thing, Pussy swollen from the constant pounding. Living in the glow of the false reflection—self on earth, alone.

I ask too many questions of eternity, he says. I open my mouth to reply, and it is met with a closed hand. I think back to the day I found the strength to leave him to his world of ice. His face—pure pallor—stone in a sea of white flakes, raining down as gently as my peace had come to me from nowhere. I had in me a dormant resolve, set on fire.

The enigma that was Nicholas Bezalel had calcified, attaining some archaic permanence that was impossible to break. The once jolly glint in his eye suggests constant mockery. His smile, although stunning under the stage lights and as wide as ever, decidedly sinister—pallor and the gauntness cheeks, all haunting. One would assume that twenty years had passed, rather than eight. What I once regarded as his transient darkness had become a permanent fixture. Undoubtedly his idealism remained, but whether or not it had taken an insidious turn, I simply cannot know.

But don't I?

He presses the thin knife to the skin beneath my breasts, between my ribs. The skin flinches at the touch—cold metal, a finger of dark fortune, sliding from place to place.

"Is this the way it should be?" he asks. Nothing falls from me. Not words, but terror. I know this court of chaos—his mind in ecstasy. It is no place for me to be safe. I have never felt more powerless. More alone. He drops the knife to the floor. "Keep it," he tells me, and leaves the room. I feel my mother, my grandmother, the great mothers of unconscious time screaming.

He walks around in the daze of loving me, but believing this as it is would be a mistake. I think like this, in permanence, because some things thrust in my direction can't be real. Am I not in dread of life as much as he? Did I not stand aloft, before the markings, accountable as myself? Did I not love Von Aurovitch as much as he? Did I not see that he loved me, and decide the same for my own reasons? The blame for evil must be put upon the self as much as outward. I would have walked away, had I had a mind for preservation. I spin and retch and revel with this chaotic heart of mine. There is dead sound there. An absence of love where I say that it is so. Will I not pay for this as strongly as he will for all he does? Some fates are intertwined in devastation, but not doom. There may be some living purpose to the gross entanglement of hearts. Even with the spouting of black and the dribbling of hateful blue. I am Anonyma. The every-girl. I see and I have seen, and they will, too.

Clouds gather in the corridor of daydreams. I am suspended in pink foam again. I have no need for such conversations. Words are confusion. The tools of deep mistrust. I whirl in worlds of silence in my heart. Touch and touch alone as seeds of feeling. When we sit in ways like this, I have no doubt. No fear. In his eyes there was forgiveness. In quiet arms, eternal peace.

Is it Nicholas? Could it be? Or some strange mirage of man? A fit of the old master's hand and mine, conjuring up some figure from the deep?

Nicholas wishes to penetrate the higher essence of my existence. To drain me of that magnificent unknowable element that I do not know myself. An earl of falsehood, tongue-tangled in the eruption of black locks on my head.

I live in a colorless anxiety, envying golden death. All doves rot under the eye of time. I have not traveled lightly.

With a reliance on God because I cannot rely on myself in this weakness, I ask only this. That I be reborn in my skin as the strongest bird of fire—that I may emerge from this dust, all I was ever meant to be. The seed of this state is buried deep. I know it lives inside, somewhere, though years of journeys seeking outward led me astray. I come to the wall of the abyss as close to the bottom as those perilous times. How it has come to be again, I have no idea. I hope that I will not need to know all of that. I do hope I can remember how to climb out.

He spits into my hair. Then the rest of them follow suit. The warm tendrils of goo run down over my painted face. I would cry out, but this is *my* predicament. It would not make sense to many why this continued. But they do not know the prescient stink of loathing when it faces inward. That is not to say that there is no resolve, pounding out from the inner chambers of my chest, screaming. He will not prove it to the earth. He will not prove it to the stars. He will not prove it to the spirits lurking over. They know my name.

CHAPTER NINE

BEZALEL APPROACHES THE four figures. They are wearing black hooded robes. Their faces are not visible. One of the figures hands a set of robes to Bezalel. He begins to remove his suit to put them on.

Bezalel, in black robes and flanked on both sides by two of the robed figures, approaches from a distant part of the room. The echo suggests some vast hall or auditorium. Lying on the floor is the actress who played Ariette. She is naked and covered in scratches, bruises, and blood. Her wound has been bandaged, but it appears that it will eventually be fatal. She breathes shallowly, drifting in and out of consciousness. Bezalel and the figures stop in front of her, now illuminated by some unseen light source. Bezalel looks quite different yet again. His hair is a mess, his eyes are glassy and sunken, and his skin is pale. Bezalel is menacing.

Two of the figures take out a cryptic-looking crown with vast, dark horns upon it. They place it upon Bezalel's head, completing his evil attire. The actress stirs, letting out a painful moan as she reaches a more wakeful state. Bezalel looks at her and smiles slightly. The figures stand tall behind him as he looks down at her. The first figure to Bezalel's right reaches out and throws a fistful of dirt on her body. Bezalel looks at him and laughs slightly. It seems they share some private joke. The girl writhes as the dirt enters her wounds. The man to Bezalel's immediate left shifts nervously.

Bezalel leans down and runs his hands over the body of the girl. She can be no more than seventeen. Tears run down her face as he runs his hands down her stomach and towards her groin. She lets out a loud moan as he reaches his hand into her private parts. He stands again and reaches his hands out. The lights flicker. One of the figures hands Bezalel a long knife. He closes his eyes, holding it and concentrating deeply. He then leans down and whispers in the girl's ear. The girl closes her eyes and nods weakly, mouthing the word "yes." Bezalel runs one hand down her chest and stomach again, running the knife behind it slightly on her skin. It does not cut her, but the cold makes her hyperventilate and flinch in expectation.

He continues to run the knife up and down her body, being careful not to cut her. He is teasing her with the thought of butchery. Bezalel begins to cut her from the groin to her stomach. Blood pours from her.

I ask him where he has been this night. There is no answer. Thunder from the distant mountains. There are no windows. He looks into my eyes, and earth, no longer firmly rooted, will fade like so many stars into the abyss.

I stand before the worst of them, if prior taunts were honest. Memory flames shot between teeth. I will speak no more, not wanting to live. I can still see the milky water running down my face. Taste its gentle salts—feel the cold rush wash over my youthful chest. I come back to reality amid this mess, without feeling.

He tells me a story of a tree, deep in the desert, with five enormous wings.

He says, "do not believe the worst," but I have known the worst of men. Unforgiving in their joys, the breeding ground for ignorance.

In my seat, a memory woman screams my name. Not my given name, with all its bells and burdens, but the one I have not heard in years. I remember.

There is no noble love beneath the hate of God. I met them in the dark years, knowing then that I was in over my head. He'll spit in the sacred place under heaving stars. Might they fill my womb with the batter of the firmament, wrapped in velvet? Tongues sink into spider rings. A tyrant of the deep. Purity cooked under lights of deep red. I am always received as one of them.

Nights of lovely piano sounds are replaced with bloody vomit.

I look at him without love. He does not know me. There is no mask of nonsense so effective. Drawn back in agitation (or love), I dance a dream of passionate death for eons in my seat. It would be an absurdity, to love me. A deficient always in a daze, with quiet, muffled depths like frozen oceans. Only those whose love is treacherous and vague may find their way to the side of me. Even then, there is no nourishment for the body or the mind. I lean towards the precipice of life and death, always mixing glitter with these scars of mine.

I grow weary of the war within. He tells me that he loves me and my faith has turned to fog. He runs his teeth and tongue over me, eyes of greed becoming of madness. I am dead at heart, as much as the first day. I remember his fingers in my mouth—once sweet, passionate. Now they graze my lips with that alien aggression.

I look at my gentle face. The delicacy, the innocence of that time. I mourn for that girl, as I mourn for any girl wandering in this world with magic in their hearts and hell in their eyes.

His laugh had the cadence of birdsong. Evil is soundless, I tell myself. This cocoon of menace fondles me tighter. I strain my eyes between two faces. One fresh, one fractured.

False comforts are counted on high. This, either enchanted puzzle or despairing labyrinth, weighs heavily without definition. I grant myself love in gushes, just to taste a sliver of the real. I wish myself endlessness in the morning. Privacy, protection, rest. I live in dread of the light that will wake him across the city. It is not a fatal blow. This is his decision. I am alive.

CHAPTER TEN

I AM ANONYMA. This I will remember in the darkest moments. I send the remnants of myself up into the clouds, to hover over bloodless hearts and tearless torment. In this way, I will live beyond these moments. I know that I will start again someday.

Nicholas speaks of his old wish, but I will not listen anymore. I am tired of the pursuit of power. His rage is rooted. He can't fathom a woman being so profound. Not in history, not before him now.

He ties the barbed wire around my arms, yanking them every third loop to set the edges in deep. Blood and sperm poured from my lips—the numbness and swelling making it impossible to close them. This is dark magic. This magic has darkened me.

Are you ever a woman until you feel the pain of she?

I remember it all, as clearly as I see this place—thousands of headstones laid out before my eyes. Lives as rich as mine. Lives as empty. All the in-betweens. I wonder what another may have done in that mess. Then I think to myself that I lived this because only I was meant for such a thing. How hard that is to fathom. That alone, we are born to know such horrors intrinsic to ourselves. Our blood. Our cells.

I want to believe that he loves me, but love to a man is a very different concept. I think it is, primarily to them, a strain of possession. In the case of Nicholas, this is true. I cannot speak for other men, really. I have not known them. I have only known this hammer upon my head. This burden of the heart. Even in my unfamiliarity with all things passionate and intimate, I know this is not love.

I want to be a mother, but perhaps it is not meant to be. I can tell by my mind and the nightmares of failure in that regard. He pines for the blue lady, and I am tired of the fascination. I see only myself in her fading form, longing to escape the peering eyes of men.

In a dream, I leave the bridge, soul intact, my cloak dragging through the snow in streaks of soul blood. Red, purple, black. Stripe after stripe leading a trail of darkness behind me.

"What mist is this that crowds my eyes with melancholy?"

He speaks, and I know it to be false concern. My stomach screams in the twisted agony. Ecstasy and horror. He who once was death, in flesh, has returned with all the glory of the resurrection.

I have translated the passage for him. The ritual will be dark—decadent. A host of spirits from the eight parallel worlds, hovering in the slipstreams—waiting for me, though I will not see them there. This was his dark design at its most precious.

Delicate veils hide demonic faces. The forest trembles, electricity rumbling through every beech and oak. Bark peels, branches curl. Smoke erupts from the belly of the mutilated goat. A bleeding hand—mine—reflects in the stillness of its eyes. This is not my work. This is not my life.

I ask madness, "what of these enchantments? These illusions? These lies?"

I lick the blue bones of his hand, and he responds with a question. I respond with the only thing I can say in this world.

"No."

With the burden of my senses magnified in this colorless company, I know myself to be at the mercy of gray souls. Though to assign some supernatural significance to my own brought me to the edge of vomiting. I am nothing. I am nothing. I am nothing. This I knew in earnest, pinching flesh. But as myself, untouched—a soul, cradled by voiceless voices from some sacred beyond—I know myself to be something. Not better or worse than the rest. Not special. Only predestined for horror and magnificence in turns. In this way, I could be nothing and not be ashamed. This is but the earth, after all.

Coreya stands by the mangled white oak, carving sigils into the trunk with her pocketknife. Nicholas has disappeared to some shadowed edge of the forest to gather his senses (or senselessness).

Ignatius stretched like a deranged lamb in the center of the clearing, flocked by Marina, Rai, and Leilan. The others linger, watching every length and limb of me so that I stand no chance of escape.

The old goat, blind with a decided limp, is carried to the circle by Mars. Two baby goats are led on leashes to the circle.

"But... I thought but the one would..."

"Three sacrifices, my love. That is the way of this."

They cut the throat of the goat, and the gash spills blackest blood.

His rituals are endless, but I am not forced. I am equally accountable, aren't I?

The angels are not absent, only sleeping.

Lithe prayers reach into the night, up unto sapphire clouds.

I am consumed by reserve. This evil is my doing.

He tells me that I owe him, but a dead thing owes no one.

We need no priests here. No pomp and circumstance.

He has the look of Von Aurovitch. The high cheekbones, watery blue eyes, and curly platinum hair. They shared a dark, whimsical charisma, particularly powerful in the company of evil. Tonight, they could be the same man.

I am anonymous. I shed the air from my breast and reach to stroke wings that aren't there. Becoming smaller, wilted, ash and nothing. I remember trembling with anger. The others pant and discharge their regrets. The ritual hasn't worked this time, they spit. I feel a growing enormity—the amphitheatre of the heart. They are wrong. They simply did not see as one must see. As one happens to see by chance. In the pandemonium of the nightmare orgy, all eyes are turned away from me. No one sees my fragile feet lift from the soil, hovering in the bluish half-haze of broken time. The light against the womb, in my eyes.

He walks over to me. Through him I feel the dense weight of earthly loss. Saturated with the whims of feminine meditation. The crowd thins and the girls grow paler. I feel the storm of life pressed against my stomach. A birth that will pierce a thousand veils of light, soaking a warm July night with lunar fascination. I hold his poor, profane face in my hands. He touched his lip to mine—their inhuman softness pulsing. The ancient paradox of nature holds me back. Ornaments and objects as preternatural wonder.

About to pull the knife from wrist to throat, I realize that my home is in myself.

Walking home, alone, I am a woman under a mass of stars. This thick deceit of flesh throbs with a beating. I roll myself in red waves—as dead as dead can be. Grass and vines reach out to hold my hand as I pass the river in the heart. Where have I gone? I am not in this empty house. I am not in this empty life. Asking with the fullness of infinity, knowing good things in the dust can't venture far.

For little girls who know they live in worlds far from their own.

I've danced with men I didn't love and cried in want of those who would not be mine. I step on my own wetness on the stairs and know the gestation of the heart has been fatal. I feel the madness in my body live again.

CHAPTER ELEVEN

THE APPARITION OF our future slumps beside me on the bed. I am his wife in name-only. My husband is fresh with memory. His heart races. Empty eyes perform ritual sweeps—fantasy-love, a splinter of the real.

"I love you as much as I am able to love a person."

I imagine years beyond this. Our daughter retreats into her room, awake with the earth, asleep in the universe. He moves dispassionately around her, an opaque vision of a child that *should-have-been*. My silence bursts open, mouth gleaming with the silver haze of distance. I am in love, without myself.

Golden light gleams on white morning walls. I step outside the front door, undressed, lost to the sickness. People stare. My husband is not here. They see the heart-wounds, oozing black salt, the smell of sulfur. Ghosts are morning-born, beside me. I feel the urge—the heat of the earth-guiding me as I fall.

"I love you as much as I am able to love a person."

Scraping sounds surround me—midnight hounds clawing against broken glass. I flinch and awaken in a storm of teeth-gnashing, snarling, dripping saliva onto my breasts.

The sky is black. A fissure breaks in the distance. Wind stirs golden leaves up in amethystine light. My mind oscillates through the fears of my heart—succumbing to doom-design—the mythic feature of the *Scaearulldytheraeum*.

I am without a body as the teeth fade into the mist. Liquid washes over my skull. My gaze falls to my wrist, blossoming red vines that move like newt tails. They glow and shrivel, dropping away from me. The scar is a glistening patch of skin—ivory velvet to the touch. I have one memory of myself—a glasswork phoenix in black lamplight, and I awaken, as cold as death—rising from the bed without emotion.

The last letter of luxury in the ailing house is the clawfoot bathtub. Dark mold crawls up the aging porcelain in places where, underneath the weight of a house mother's hand, there may have been a striking glow. There will be no such care in this house.

Sick eyes stare into the mirror again. I hold the razor's edge to my jet-black hair and take three violent cuts. Once-flowing locks are now blunt tendrils, falling above the ears. My hair has a 20s-flapper look to it, if a flapper had ever been caught in a woodchipper. I peer into the drain at the lost strands of black, clotted together in a damp mass of dream-blood.

Rusty pipes rattle as I draw the bath. My hand touches the porcelain and I shudder—a momentary fragment of *real life*. The breakthrough is not enough. As I place my fingers beneath the faucet to feel a growing warmth, I recall my mother as she recounted the tale of her Great Aunt's near-drowning as a child. Exhausted from swimming in the worst heat of the season, she began to succumb to the depths of the lake. The peculiar part of the recollection had always been the music she heard that soothed her as she sunk below the surface. A gentle, calming song that could only have been from heaven itself, or so she proclaimed. Her father rescued her before she drowned, and she lived to tell the tale to her many relatives, including mother, who was petrified of water.

I press the cold blade tip against my chest and know I am loved by this coldness. If nothing else, in blood, in light, I know it by the kiss of killing metal. I believe I will be blessed with a particular uselessness after all.

I have no fear of water. I slip into its warmth. A pale, nude figure, obscured beneath the gentle rippling, grows more still with each breath. Pressing the razor against my inner arm, I trace a gentle line vertically down to my wrist, where the cut will go. I press again, and watch flesh burrow up around the metal.

My death procession is bright red. Slipping down down down into the bathwater. Everything I decide is usurped by tiredness. I rebel inwardly against myself, in dread of love, knowing only a veil of weakness, the march of theatric fright. I fool even myself without ferocity, but it is there. Buried deep—a fathomless strength beneath every fitful sob. My eyelids drop as I remember him. Might a cascade of dust fall out of his nostrils, revealing himself to the world? My eyes sink into the pool of impossibility. There is no music.

I recall the act of trembling in the arms of a madman. Powder pink roses sit on his desk. Terror blooms—a blanket of pus, dampening the memory—the refuge that was once shared lives. He is no longer familiar. Every spoken word, a stranger. Every glance inflames the senses. The depths of a yellow autumn and wafts of mold creep up from the old floorboards. Beauty was once there, but in the crazy swarm of routine, the fever of dreams, I had to make the attempt. Eternally sad in a dream of motherhood, deep-set eyes weeping. His coffin, no doubt, would smell of tea and mine of a weeping womb. I broke through this submission, taking ownership of myself.

I am in the jaws of the afterlife without having fulfilled my earthly promises. It is in this way that one feels a sense of guilt when the blood pours out. I had not the courage for the convulsions one receives from poison. One slice to the arm, and I was whisked into a scented, spaceless night. He rushed into the room. His cold hand presses against my neck. Dark blood sputters up like spirit larvae. I wander in the artist's semi-darkness, green blood gushing and all manner of mind game stretching beyond the alien comforts of calm weather. I can feel him there, but it is too late.

In Nicholas Bezalel, I recognize the darkest part of myself. Feel his dark energy, at once vulnerable and outraged, as I cross over. The delicate strain of old torment, wondering why such a thing has to be. Why I have failed him once again. His throat bellows out the tune of furious dreams. The cold dignity is lost from his face. His brow, weighed down with pride, shocks the air with the filth of his inner universe. That is not to say that he is incapable of love. Of lovingness. Only that his heart has become a distant forest, where gray whispers wilt in a ceaseless dullness. The last thing I see before the dark pull is the fear drawn into every facial feature. A deep draft as lifeblood pours into the bath, into his hands. The candles blow out. Naked and overpowered by dark chaos, feeling the fabric of his coat as he pulls me out of the water, I succumb to the world of the half-dead, as intended.

There is a phantom severity that even he could not have predicted. Bezalel cradles my cooling body on the floor, weeping over the predicament. He has loved others deeper but had never known this gentle resolve.

I awaken in another world as a higher version of myself. No different in appearance or mind. Only in gravity. A lightness of body that likens itself to a gentle dream. I mark the manner of this gentleness and knows it as deceit. A dream-complete. The true ritual. This is how it begins, in Doom-sleep.

CHAPTER TWELVE

PINK DUST LOOMS on high over the treetops. Lie down here, the wind whispers. Sleep. Sleep! Lie down here, be lulled by the leaves. Lulled deeply into sleep, pleasant sleep! But what do they want of me? Why did I go in? I have only the knowledge of partial death, tied to the sad living world by spirit threads I cannot cut.

How I have come to be here—beneath branches of lavender, roots of gold, I have no recollection. Granite eyes extend to the lord's constellation. Glorious vanity, shuddering on moist shoulders in the last known place before the woods. I mark the mangled mess of dreams and wonder.

I take pleasure in absurd insomnia, as one takes pleasure in a fine, weightless disgrace. Incapable of the fullness of life, I am only a witness to the artifice of the woods. The riverbed breathes. Blue lightning breaks the sky in pieces. Strange slurring words of untraceable language travel from the deepest reaches of the land... and human skin in piles, feast—bait for something lurking beyond my senses.

I lower my head to the emptiness of my convulsions and think, "What do I fear?" Floundering through the brush, slicing lengths of flesh—as violent and as wistful as in life. The rigid air clouds over, alien and diseased, in a matter of moments. Panic-stricken, I amble through thick, metallic mud as blackness spreads over the electric sky. Plunging into the protection of the muck as the strikes shake the treetops, I taste the insidious liquids of the forest. Alien scents shock the senses. As I emerge from the mess, I notice countless scrapes from submerged tree roots. My belly bleeds the dark wisdom of the woods.

Nicholas is out there, somewhere—spirit mandibles at the intersection of horizon and hell. Viewing restraint as silk, black hair as velvet, brilliance as precipitation. I wonder if he has taken me from the bath of blood. If he has even found my body shriveling there—the quiet aftermath. The sky bleeds its silver magic, hardening men. Horrifying me. I allow myself to be seen by this unsacred darkness, through the frigid air and firmament. I feel a kick. I am being twinned in this fragility, as hollow as the deepest mold of the earth.

The mud fades from the deep stink of metallic fumes to a frothy pink scum. There I find other men, other women—bodies soaked and sunken, in and out, tear-salted eyes glued open. My stomach, scabbed and bruised, retracts at the sounds of death emitting from their mouths.

Here drown the first subjects I will witness. My mind holds a glittering memorial to all once seen and felt outside of the woods. On approach, thirst becomes insatiable, but I know this: drink from the stream, and I will lose my mind in the erotic anguish of these vanquished spirits, soaked through with the dark dreams of deceit. Twilight urges me toward dread. Towards faintness of will. I walk forward to mourn the mob of bodies in the froth, who, without sight or hearing, will not know me. I wipe away my tears on the perfect peeled skin of the dead and return to the depths of the diseased brush. Gold roots. Blue light. Shrill piping of a sickened dawn. My tongue crawls out in want of water. There is nothing without pus or poison. Nothing untouched by the alchemical decadence of doom-design. Even this will mark me as a pariah in the Afterworld. Disobedience is accessory to ruin, even here in the woods.

I had avoided my own nakedness like death. Fought the onslaught of twisting bodies. Little flowers, my only vice, were arranged in a nighttime theatre of the heart. I hold one yellow rose to my cheek, only to watch it shrivel into dust. As we all will. My skin is flaking. With one sharp sweep of my hand, I release the dust of my flesh, snowing over the mud.

Resting against a stone, I wonder if delirium is the bird's final instinct. Finding this in myself, it is the only natural conclusion I want to come to, contemplating the immensity of death. I have forgotten my desire. And like the wilted earth forgets me, I collapse—a long fall into the field of darkest blossoms, illuminated only by my endless night.

Spirits don't stand guard over these people, and never within reach of the woods. I feel their absence in these lands, more so than on earth. But with the richness of sights so profound, so confusing, there is something of a meditation to existence only.

The stolen souls will vomit up the filth of their passion in the river. Seethe with the dark vehemence of the woods. Turn to stone as they sleep in waking life. A pale sludge will ooze from the eyes and ears, as it is in the *Scaearulldytheraeum*. The bodies collapse as such, evaporating within minutes. One must wonder at what cost such things occur. Their faces are painted with the quiet corruption of youth, and I think *where* and *why* and *how* and *who* has done this to them?

No means of confirmation sets me at ease. Only deeper into terror. With wide eyes shivering, glancing over my shoulder, I turn—nothing. Nothing to be seen, save for the missing horizon, buried in a regiment of bark and brush.

Pleasure thrives on forgotten guilt. Penetration after penetration. An orgy of sound and body, consummated in the deep mud of the riverbank. Without breath, I hide behind the thickest tree, watching. I hold my own hand as all glitters around me. Forgotten innocence in the depths of detachment. I faintly recall the sharp penetration—Nicholas Bezalel inside me for the first time. Bristles scrape my inner thighs in the dark. The gutting of the nervure like angel hair from the spine.

All sensations are lost to me but the phantom slithering. I cannot make sense of the shapes at my feet, only shapes—pale and serpentine. In the lull beneath the darkling crescent, the ecstasy of invisible insects is not lost. Heat stirs deep inside the unseen parts of me. It trickled down my legs and disappears into the mess of mud. My legs are floating, floating. I weep in this ecstasy, falling back against the somber weight of the woods.

Now I am awake. I am waking. The bodies soak in the ever-changing mud. Their bellies are bloated. I look down and see my own hyaline protrusion. A great big bulb of black glass from the mid-torso, and I get the sickly feeling. The deeper I go, the stranger it will become. Souls in installation as spirit meat—both sustenance and procreative wonderment. So even I must be brought to wonder—where is this devil who requires so much? And what use might have I, now? Who is the doom artist of the dark woods?

Platinum dust flies off the bark upon impact. A galloping sound grows as I gaze into the mist of worlds. Motionless in fear, my mind racing to the *Mare of a Thousand Wounds*, I am unable to even cover my ears from the onslaught of sound. My horizontal softness, crushed. The faint sensation of slithering returns over my toes and my darkened guts erupt with longing. This passion knows no hand or heart of man. Only the tiny life, present in some spectrum within my will to conjure. I must protect her from all of this *death*.

CHAPTER THIRTEEN

FALLEN GODS DRAW dreams on earth, in disorder. They want grace, not echoes from infinite worlds. It would be fitting that the death-divide would merge the profane and unclean with the disdainful dreams of a hateful god. In this death, it finds the erotic, the playful. Not fury or indifference. The great god's hands are unclean and not hands at all. Rather pools of hateful glaze, swimming through the elements, through me.

In my own eyes I find the quickness of life – unprepared. I continue in the fatal tradition of laughter, but a sliver of warmth ascends from gut to mouth. I emit the mass of my juices. Born in overarching filth, pink mist, and insect resin, I stumble in slow motion—as decrepit as my experiences are mediocre. Wounded by inconsistency, I cradle whispers as children and hurl them towards the eternal landscape.

Looking up to a sea of stars, one planet sits in orbit of this dream existence. One blue world without a name, always hovering.

A gentle white powder graces my face and chest, soothing the senses, warming the surrounding air. I have emerged from the woods. In spite of everything, I feel a quiet bliss raining down, in anticipation of the night. I was born a great dreamer. Tormented within by the halls of possibility, braving the earth with the sensation of absolute failure. Gleaming, stretching, glittering worlds exist beyond the bounds of the body. This flesh, the artifice of God, himself dead, floating in the loveliness of crumbling statues and bleeding bodies.

A vengeful gale rushes past; a streak of yellow sailing into the black ignominy of the heavens. Each moment brings a new heaviness to the chest and face. From the paralysis of love, I grow silent, seeing only flocks of dark birds gather over a sea of petulant slime.

With acidic wrath that could disintegrate metal, a bath of pain as warm as terror's inverse. Miraculous sucking! Delirious moon! The gray flags wave in the ships like insects in file to oppression.

A column of rain frightens the scarlet serpents lingering at my feet. A sharp gale throws my body against blonde grass, terror swimming through still blood.

The procession of ships moves carefully through the currents, unable to move with ease over the waves of slime. A splintering white dock emerges in the distant fog, revealing cloaked travelers from every vessel, carrying bone lanterns of strange green light. Captured will-o'-the-wisps or some other such creature, in anger, flickering over the currents and onto the dunes.

One such passenger from the lowly ships approaches me, cloaked in purple, face obscured by both hood and mask of metal.

"You are the visitor in Doom-sleep?" it asks, the hissing tone of his voice hurts my ears.

"I am," I answer.

It motions towards the dock. Turning in the opposite direction, I see nothing but sands turning into a valley drowning in blonde grass and buried serpents. Hesitating, I turn back and follow him to the dock.

Closer inspection reveals the ships to be perilous. Dead bodies attached to giant hooks sit in single-file rows. I turn to run but am halted by the robed creature, elephantine face now visible after the unlatching of its metal coverings.

"One can cross the sea intact," he begins, motioning for me to sit. I remain standing. "But madness awaits them." I examine the nearest body. A young girl, dark skin, tawny-haired and fragile, the hook dug deeply into her lower abdomen. No blood.

"Is she living?"

The creature points skyward. I look and see a hovering translucence over the ship. Feel a shower of life rain down upon me.

"Joined again on the other shore. Yes, they live."

Nodding, the creature holds the white hook to my eyes, then sets it into my stomach without warning. White dust pours out of the wound. I lower my eyes in horror, teeth chattering, senses screaming, feeling myself being pulled backwards with alarming force—a shadow figure fading in front of me. I identify as my own body. Unable to perceive the vastness of myself, I succumb to the moisture and the journey. Floating upward in an arc, spirit tether keeping me secure. Showers of silver, streaking past the moon, reflect on the tethered spirits, all.

With pride, I thrust myself over the waves, bound to my corpse. I am not free in this state, not alive either. Though this gliding through air and foam bears something of an elemental promise. Crossing through the sea is difficult, though not a difficulty of nature. The wild, ecstatic night accompanies me through this agony of learning, and I sense a silent faith grow within my chest. Even pain-in-bones abates to the wild coos of nocturnal creatures, unfamiliar in this realm of After-Earth. Fuscous liquid thrashing—a familiar violence. Monumental waves soaring in impossible directions, menacing gales from the dead heavens, the faint glow of enormous sea worms ebbing in and out of the currents, bashing the side of the ship in territorial rage.

After endless hours, the faint outline of a structure looms in the distant night. A giant gold cube, supported by an angled disc, emerging from slime.

Demon eyes dilate upon the scene—absurd illusions. All familiar and growing. The cube, upon closer inspection, glows with a rubiginous hue. We reach the dark shore of the heathen place. I emerge from the ship wearily; raven hair curling from dampness and humidity. An anemic bird-like creature, albino and neurotic—huddles by the palace door, caked in mildew and algae, counting fungi sprouting from golden plaster.

Floating ghouls carry giant orange worms with a thousand legs from the slime. A fisherwoman, slowed by her pendulous breasts, shaven head gleaming in the light of the rising moon, drops a worm, approaches me. Dreadful sounds ring out from the doorway. A phantom ebb of lurid notes. Haunted songs for a haunted scene. The fisherwoman watches as I float back into my body. Once rejoined, she hurls me onto the dune. Struggling to stand, she points to the enormous, rotting doorway. I stand, limping to the entryway, averting my gaze from the hideous creature pricking his claws on splintered driftwood.

The intestinal halls of the gold cube palace lead to an enormous chamber. Azure draperies, like waterfalls, cascading down over ivory stone. I stride along in earnest as cloaked servants writhe and gesticulate towards their master, sitting atop a mangled green throne.

Red eyes gleam madness at leisure. The electric monotony of human genius. A tall, wretched forehead, yellowing grimace, fingers made of smoke that fail to grasp. His face, drawn close to mine, radiates a disease of wealth. In eras on earth all too familiar, he may have been a transcendent figure. Waves of copper heat tear through me. Growing wild with fever, I collapse to the cold floor. He speaks with an explicit artificiality—A trickster, with all the trappings of a hidden minacious temper.

"Opsimathette!" he yells to me.

I forget my imagination and hear rustling behind me. Great gales quiet outside. Throats struggle to swallow. Limbs squirm through vast labyrinths; homeless corridors of a forgotten cosmos. Words become nothing. Danger, as fantastic and exaggerated as my sleeping self, bleeds into their eyes... the eyes behind me. Those that see me as I am. Terrifying visions are born. I spiral down into this gallery of doom and turn around to see eight women standing in a line. All silent, consumed by velleity, carrying delicate carved boxes of considerable delicacy.

My eyes sweep through the line. Feeling a new weight in my hands, I look down to see my hands grasping a dull gray box, tendrils of gold leaf gathering around polished edges. Prince, or King, or Emperor before me, he is a horror of a thing. Hardly man, but string and bone, looming over these women and myself with cryptic glances. Presiding over the chamber are numerous ghosts, whispering the nonsense of sea worms, songs of inverted memory, the lust of leeches and fetid groans.

"What is this sea of muck?" I ask, eyes wide, unprepared for any answer.

"Do you not know?"

None of us are enchanted by his presence. We have long been immune to such foolishness. This I can only assume. Every one has the wide eyes Bezalel loved. The long locks, delicate limbs. That is the aftermath of worrisome affections. The peculiar monarch assumes my thoughtlessness and voluntary submission.

"In these lands I am no more than a beast," I say, "fit for servicing and discarding, is this correct?"

One woman stirs. An act of praise, or surprise at my ability to speak. Cupresous locks like the ladies of age-old paintings, striking cheekbones carved of stone. I watch her face closely, though she will not meet my eye. I know her. Here is this difficulty beyond-measure. To exist as oneself when oneself is self-haunted. I refer to the haunt of memories. Autura's features burst with archaic elegance. She is not as I am, and yet is entirely so. Better in every way, yet somehow, vague glances capture a fragment of familiarity. She is not as I am, though I am as she was, once. A beautiful woman, serious and self-possessed. Doused in the juices of hybrid sexuality. Her helplessness bears complications. An ever-present fear of glory. The delicate impressions of young life serve to mark her. She carries melancholy with a singular reluctance, unlike the others, who are entirely lost to the perils of doom-sleep. I'm shocked from my remembrances by he who must not be ignored, amethystine rod smashing the floor.

"Stand in line, Opsimathette."

"Don't call me that," I reply, alarming the servants and attendees hovering over the chamber.

"What shall I call you?"

I meet his gaze. His expression droops, disenchanted by my lack of submission.

"I have no name."

"There are no creatures without titles! Women without names! Only the definite press their eyes against eternity! All the phantoms and worms of the earth could not dispute that fact..."

Losing interior sight of betrayal, my heart grows calm within me.

"I am Anonyma."

He has within him the storm of celestial reason, unwound in ancient air, breathing into the chamber. An infection of blue words and exhaustive silences grows within him.

"Anonyma."

"And who are you?"

"I am master of no-one, not horror or joy."

My cheeks burn with apprehension.

"I am a Doom Artist."

He turns his attention from me back to the women, returning to thorough interrogations and examinations of what is inside their boxes. Each of them contains a single body part, very clearly from a male. Leaning closer into the blackness of remembrances, some of the women begin to panic. I remain still, as does Autura. Glaring at her, a frightening sharpness of aspect, she gives in to momentary control. A mirage of safety lives in the distant place she projects herself into. I can see it. Can see her soul, beaming away from here.

A happy familiarity sweeps through me at the sight of her. She grows distant in what they perceive as thoughtlessness. I see her spirit dance, her gestures, gliding to the farthest reaches of the chamber, alive, delicate, primordial elegance. There is something that becomes too graceful, too resentful in her strides. In line, they can accuse no one of mystifying the Doom Artist. Cannot reveal her power, her resolve. I see her as she is. Driven to despair by the distant emptiness, she set her mind to a new philosophy. A parody of its former self, once brimming with this decided resolve regarding the conditions of life. She apprenticed her grief beneath his, but not in totality. I hear her voice speak to me without sound.

"I want only to exist as a slight tremor in the belly of those I once knew. A timeless ache, a memory, nothing more."

I feel a sharp pang in my stomach and bend over in pain. This draws the Doom Artist's attention to me again. He steps away from examining the contents of the boxes and approaches me.

"Might you look at a scroll in my presence, Anonyma?" I feel a rolling sensation in my stomach. If I carry life, this life is worried.

What must I know to save this womb-blossom from Doom Design? A miraculous illness, forgotten in the moldy pages of the book, had re-emerged in concentrated waves in the southern hemisphere of the Afterworld. This much I knew from the *Scaearulldytheraeum*. I agree to see the pages as a mother may agree to trade her life for her child's. This was, after all, what I was doing.

The chamber sinks into disease. I cannot stop reading. The night infection spreads. My eyes shift from the dissolution of gold ink to the corner shadows. I knock the scroll out of his hands. It has the tell-tale scarlet stains of wood from the Black Forest. No decree can come from there without the stench of hostility. No doubt the drippings of Dread-Tongue. The demands of another Doom Artist—one far more evil than he.

The impulse was rewarded with phantom applause, ricocheting off of the black walls. Here I am incensed and impaled. Eternal pretenders wed with downcast eyes. Blind moths unburden themselves on the rim of reason. Silent noise reels over the beams supporting the cube. I dine on detachment, marking the ignorance of endless spaces. I hold out my hands to Autura, and he slaps them down. She whispers to me, "A dead thing owes no one." He shoots her a shattering dark look and begins to read a verse aloud.

"I am the sublime minority—no delusion in the slime can wash away this truth."

Deep sorrow slips from her, into me. I, the benefactress of blood, the falsified mistress and desired sorceress of slime. I brush my hand through her long, red hair. A waterfall of scarlet strands, gliding between every finger. With the bewilderment of apparitions, the cruelty of nature, new life grows within me. She knows the universe within herself, no longer separate from its law. At irregular intervals and a touch of shimmering, the Doom Artist's madness opens her up. He continues.

"They will bury the moon, black out the sun, return the souls of earth to the black planet, Ulldythaer."

It is a pastime of gaunts, to allow for unholy remembrances, stirring up a cloud of elder evil. When this is one's amusement, there is little room for diplomacy, let alone escape. As my thoughts drift from myself to Autura, to the life I suspect lives inside of me, the Doom Artist stops reading. He mutters, disdainful of the scroll's contents himself. A voice calls out from above.

"She will give us the new slime!"

The Doom Artist examines me closely, suspicion fading. I have no biblical ambitions within me. Only a dream of silence. Of an adjusted peculiarity, at home somewhere uncharted, as yet undiscovered. Safe and at peace. Few could guess at the extent of my seriousness. Laughter bursts from the ghouls, pale eyelashes fluttering with each wince of hideous noise. My tongue grows heavy, stopping speech as readily as fright had on earth. I imagine waking, an unhappy return into the realm of colorless life. Eyes reset, opening on my white breasts covered in blood, Bezalel on top of me, beating my body back into life. Most women know this stain in the book of eternity. She who obeys the profane rules knows no freedom, no escape. To be impure is to be alive, and there is no guilt in that racket.

The Doom Artist abruptly places a hand on my stomach. The cataclysm of the soul has passed. I feel the movement of life in me and draw a curtain on premonition. It has served for nothing but a dry ache in the tomb of my heart. Despite surgical curiosity and a frenzy of passion, I manage to hold back my inkwell of emotions. A quiet reservoir of magic lives within me that not even the slime can reach.

I fidget with the milk-white feathers that line my gown, flushing with gentle confusion. My heart bleeds an expression of profound sadness that my face fails to show.

"Why this?" he asks.

"I have adopted a fundamental indifference to all things natural." I answer, feeling unworthy, unprepared for this life.

"Many phenomena I have witnessed myself," he says, "magic in a world devoid of God."

"What will become of these women?" I interrupt, drawing his attention away.

"They will be dispersed, Noyade."

Terror freezes my throat as his expression fizzles into regret. The women lower their heads, spitting out the misery of the sky. The chapel of his heart is emptier than theirs. Bitterness and damnation, followed by the tenderness of foolish dreams. But dreams should not be this way, should they? A hideous heart trembles the inverted sky and memories become treasures, lost to time. Deep cackling rains down from the firmament. Fear seeps into the features of the Doom Artist. He ushers me towards the hallway.

"Go."

"No, you can't disperse them!"

I look to Autura, the only one not yet trembling. The soul-fear soaks her limbs in distress. She can no longer move them. The night has reached her organs.

"If my name is despair, am I not a conqueror of novelty? Human lives have little value here, unless they are carriers."

He looks down to my stomach again. A great shadow passes the northern cathedral window. The skies darken, sounds of flapping circling the cube with phantom curiosity. Fear flashes in his eyes. The Doom Artist remains still until the sound fades and light returns to the chamber. He walks me outside with a guiding force that prevents me from turning back. I ache for Autura, for the others.

"Please," I plead. "Let them live."

He walks me to the ship and lifts me in, setting the hook within me himself, as though it is a privilege. The Doom Artist blows a kiss to the dark horizon as snow and sand intermingle at his feet. I look at him one last time.

"Let them live."

For a moment, his façade washes away, revealing deep exhaustion. After a sigh, he replies.

"A dead thing owes no one."

The sea of slime has changed color. Once a sickly green, it now exudes an earth-like tone of blue. The surface glistens with orange crystals and ivory threads—alien vegetation. The worms have grown quiet. I recall the contents of the sacred boxes on the journey. One girl holds a hand, one an ear. Another a penis. Autura's contained a heart. Mine remains sealed.

I whisper gentle inanities to myself, kissing the surface of the curious box and throwing it into the sea. I have no desire to know its contents. The remnants sink. Loam froths up like soap bubbles from the slime. Looking back, I see the white banks traversed by unknown emperors disintegrate in the tidal thrush. In the distance, the great gold cube pivots on its edge. Artlessness, being too common, brought about the rigor of the rising tide. Ghastly ice blocks dangle from the twisted scaffolding that protect the cube from elemental decay. The balcony breaks away. Swallowed by the sea of slime, creeping back into its crestless ease as though nothing had happened.

With all I have, I have not seen, and yet am still entirely myself. I am young, thoughtful on the threshold of the strange world, but will not die of grief.

The old monotony is lost to me now. I wear the silk of my dead sisters, thinking it allows them to breathe somewhere far from here. I feel a sense of my old self stirring. Smell the roots of autumn, waking. Taste the tongue of the green lady. Eat the fear of worms. Whisper songs of the dark firmament as though these texts had meant nothing to me at all.

Here I would not know, but strive to know. Here I would be familiar with things unfamiliar, experience the repeated monotony expected of all, and shame would fall between every crack of the soul exposed to inclement internal weather. In the denouement of death, the body will have been enough. When sickly and when wretched, enough. Tired, unwell. Enough.

Here, a frail flower. Here, cold death. A dead God haunts the breast of innocence. There he lives and breathes anguish beyond repair. His vanity was infinite, to be planted in women and men, stirred by lightning, calmed by wind, reflected in the belly, gleaming in the head. The divine absence burns up the light of a thousand tombs and lives again. A bird escapes the flames, the debris of death, and soars into the whiteness of the infinite night. His heart is hardened. Hers, delirious. Vomit drips from their noses and evaporates. A pale mouth presses against hers. Her eyes roll back, intoxicated, choking, pus and no air, no air. She reawaken on the ship, greater than dust, with a stirring thirst for pink roses.

CHAPTER FOURTEEN

EVERYTHING IS LOST in the somber contemplation wreaking from the slime. The soul becomes enormous in its presence. Uncontainable. One can only reconcile themselves to the shadow's antithesis: a memory of light, elsewhere.

I have come to a place on the outskirts of the shore. A crystal palace, wrapped in mud. Where once were severed heads on spikes, now hover bodies in glass. Wisps of life, as lanterns, in the darkness. Tangled up as monstrous artifice—conscious of their misfortune and knowing only one ending. These are ghosts in motion—through thoughts and dreams, as violent and undiminished as the wind. The works of another Doom Artist.

I know she as myself because they have said I am this, this is me.

They bury their faces in sickness. The glow fades in, and out, and in, and out—a distant lightning in the procession of storms. I stand in the corner beneath them, watching the swaying of forms without full comprehension. Breath is frail—a fading defiance. Naked, pale, limply hanging—stiffness of limbs, bones merged with glass, cracked lips, murmurs, moans and calloused fingertips, bursting. That's the worst of it. It means they will never touch another person—in passion or in pain—again. From the waist down, there is nothing but shredded flesh, flowing as tattered muslin may. With each brain-stem tethered to long, serrated needles as sinister as any machine, there will be no movement back or forward. Nothing but the eternal floating that has thusly been assigned above the web. In times of distress, heads tilt down to look at the delicate strands. The vibrations carry through their skulls, easing every thought and pain into a dreary pulse.

I am she because they see me as she.

There is no tincture so deadly as bias without sleep. The only sound is the delicate clicking of a blood drop, falling mouth to mouth, nourishing the ghoulish web watchers. A single drop falls on my lips, and I taste the sorrow of the universe. Muscles contract in passion's inverse. Saliva dribbles from each gaping maw. Against a jagged fragment of bone, flesh strings and intestines tangled—they sense themselves to be the last alive, suspended above the imperial scurrying. Threads of dreams, spun out like the darkest of the wicked arachnid's web, glisten with static drops. Bloated, glistening tubes like rotting flower stems outside the gates of the Silver City. Hate is imprecise, but it has found a home here.

I am not she because I am she.

Sleeplessness is the will-killer. Suspended in the electric cradle, they lose might with each growing shock, awake to their own dismemberment. Skeletal waists, still intact but heavy with sickness, ache with the eternal sensation—instinct. A strange ecstasy bleeds into the air. The temptation of disgust. They watch through bloody eyes, the web without relief, lids ripped and gone. They see the punishment for living—bodies dragged from floor to ceiling, pressed to the needles, left to rot above the sparkling web alongside them as imperial decoration. They become aware of beauty as malformation, its wickedness the preserver of revulsion. Condemnation throbs—the old tradition. Chants of unrest are silenced by severed tongues, but language alone is not life.

All is numb in this sky of impossibility. Broken bodies—vessels of flesh through which one experiences the earth—keep living. Keep living.

I am she without myself, because this is not me.

Men who deal in dreams should know better or know nothing at all. Captive hearts, in glass. I imagine toothless gums in infancy, teetering on the edge of the web, pouring drool. It pours and pours, cascading over the woven strings like liquids of passion on porcelain flesh.

I am not she. I am not he. Should I be? Should I be? This is what they tell us. What they tell me. But I am not one of these.

The metal clanging continues behind the cathedral wall. In the unknown hours, I expect Saturn himself to emerge after the devouring of his children, breaching the wall to set down upon faultless bodies with his deadly enormity. As they do with the web. As they do with the earth. What other enormity could commit such crimes against the living? Only a Doom Artist. Worse and worse they get. Small spirits climb the golden beams, scratching. They teach the survivors how to speak without tongues to each other, that everything will be ok, that there is a life beyond this. But is there?

There is ritual below them—beside me. Ritual and concentration. Heavy with rotting, like morality. So often it is in these God-soaked places where the shaft between dirt and dollar is so poignantly felt. The web-watchers—ghouls of spite, gaunt and disheveled in their frayed, yellow robes— say there is no God for them, but they have only known lost energy in these broken places. A thousand eyes scream the error of the dreaded Imperium. Those who birth magic in opposition live on in this world.

Ghostly eyes peer out from the silver mist beyond the web. It takes only three days of the guttural emptiness for me to realize their souls sail on the threads of the colossal web—no longer in the confines of a fleeting body—beyond the hatred of earth and interpretation.

Great black Ghouls line the southern ridge. The crystal tower gleams betwixt the sea and sun. People scurry in every direction away from the breath of black magic. Something is coming.

I feel the loss of myself in the deep shimmer of the fields.

Strange voices chirrup—gentle warnings against the soil. I come to an abandoned train car, hovering over limerock tracks.

The train car is suspended in a fetid stillness. Emerald air soaks the atmosphere in toxins. Wild, grotesque—the perfume of death wades in and out of my nostrils. I am safe here, seeing through the eyes of the Iedeen, a savior of invisible light.

There are beasts aplenty in these lands, but none so horrid as those from the black moon of Ulldythaer. With elongated face like shorn rams, black teeth, and a heathen-gait, the Uldred-keind are the emissaries of evil from the outer firmament. I have learned such things, woven in black ink, from the book.

A procession of armored Uldreds enters the train car. I come to believe they are of a higher kind, having never known them to step on foot. I can see through the shattered window. An Uldred officer ejects a long pane of pointed glass from his weapon and thrusts it forward, decapitating a dying woman. The wounds in her stomach begin to grow teeth, as does the flesh dangling off of her neck. She is dispersed with orange powder.

I wriggle free of the Iedeen's protection in a daze. Blood oozes from my tears, tiny particles of powder dancing over my lids. It is now that I learn of the great terror of the Afterworld.

My spirit leaps from lamb to anguish. Angel-Lord Menchen, twelve eyes soaring apart, leads the immortal demon Uldreds to the landscapes of men. With dark sighs, they search the bogs for the afflicted.

They come from a place darker than any earth. His enslaved multitudes, eternally thirsty in the cold meadows, pulling snakes up from the ground for sustenance. Thunderous pounding rolls out over the hills, warning the world of his anger.

They are given their eye cages, sheaths and blindfolds, to hide their senses from the horrid Doom Artist. Few have ever dared to look. I run from the fields, eyes blurring, feet stinging, until the red noise no longer haunts my senses.

An ancient garden compels me to stop—eyes sparkling once more behind gloomy brush, blinded by the hard, the clear, the silent—by that which lurks and flees in fear. The Angel-Lord reaches down with scarlet God-hands as the moon grows dark. Sacred flowers wilt in his presence. Darkness sinks into the great expanse, child-worms shriveling in the wind beneath wings of old roots, chilled of inner life. They are golden, they are afraid—they are glimmers of the absolute deep. Green cocoons break open, bells sound from afar under red clouds. I hide from them.

I hide as the deep rumbling forces bitterness into my ears. There are those that say that the darkest of things remain silent. I remember moments in this way. The onslaught of hostile forces breaking me, my body, my heart, and mind without noise. But here, as I contemplate evil and blood, my eyes try this demon scene. I hear something like a song from the firmament—the rabid cry of those who watch from other places with heavy laden eyes, crystal breath, and hope within their breasts. The Afterworld is a fortress of horror. They spread their black decay through the night, through the day. Those who live in grace will perish beneath these arches, their souls shimmering in one last gush of light, without sound.

CHAPTER FIFTEEN

THE STARS ARE motionless over the forest—a silent chamber of madness. Spirits stare out as I traverse the blue wood. The wrath of God bleeds down through the thickets. I shudder, holding the memory of our dead child against me. Blood runs down her throat. My soul dreams of other things. Our father. Our village. The black bird tapping against the window of her bedroom,

I was told I have a sister*daughter* in the world. They have yet to find her. The young boy in town said she was caught up in a fence, her long locks tangled between posts.

Sister*daughter* likes the apple orchard. The thrill of natural life.

Rats plod over the cold ground, as lost as she. Bells toll without sound. In age, she may find herself a woman of smiling madness, eyes heavy with all that has been read and sought.

She is my sister*daughter*.

In prior autumns, I have been nearer to death. Shadows with silver voices broke reason. Eyes of ice and gold passed by in judgment. I dream of a bright, warm day. The fiery browns of autumn. The warmth of bread and blues of wind. The cows sleep. The birds sleep. The bugs sleep. I couldn't accept such a sanctuary as my own.

A dark saber of light swells in the distance. Like cloud rooms on high, all has come back to me, desolate and backwards. The light is weak. It breathes through the treetops, so dark that spirits sip it from the eternal overhead. But in this illusion, I confuse myself. This phantom flirting through the dark woods to retrieve my sister*daughter*. They say there are shadows here, but what of solace and gloom does not haunt forests or men? I might have known myself as less foolish then, spending more time in the woods pondering heavy thunders, and the gentle flapping of wings. I kneel for a moment in a state of wonder. What men might haunt these woods in spirit?

There is no power in me so plain that I would refuse to cheat the world with my own brand of injustice. Visions are scarce. The heart of them black, painted with light so that no one might see, but is this not the same in the hearts of men and tyrants. I pass through the woods, and it is a small treasure. A small delight. A cathedral of prayer and plants, leaves—but there is a bitterness that grows in the black light, encroaching upon me from every direction. An abysmal mystery. The curse is my side life. I find some hidden desperation exposed, and what I present is an authentic face, an authentic body. There are no mountains to poison, no seas to spit in. Only the words in eternity of one chance—one life—to make art of the dark. I have held these frustrations of mine from childhood. I speak not of such things in company. Have not spoken of them to anyone or anything. The black abyss that is the woods as a splendor of revelation—in it, I consume myself. From it, this waxing and waning of confusion sweeps. My left hand crosses my chest. I have taken hundreds of steps into the woods. I'm filthy, bloody, gold, unsure of myself. I'm unsure of the path back to the house. Dull gray light groans over the ground. I think of life as a germ—a vague sound washing through the leaves and branches. The hissing of small creatures scurrying through the leaves. Might I know some black doom in these branches? The strange voice speaks to me—approaches without feet. I wonder if I am one of these?

Visions rock me. Swelling, are these voices without bodies. These voices without names. Black sparks shoot through my chest. My eyes are bleeding, and dreadful thoughts run across the daylight. My throat aches, but I do not despair. There will be more sadness, more scarcity in life than this. I must make it home. Growing through the black wilderness, I must untangle my sister*daughter* from the fence, but with a stream of words I have lost myself. It a side effect of passion, or of ignorance. No hope can lead me towards an explanation. Only fear and fever rocks me now.

A tremulous cry is uttered. I cry out myself, but the sound is choked by the nothingness. There is a beauty in the anticipation of emergence—to be great, or to be told that things are not things. I will know nothing within the woods, and yet it is the only place I must be honest—complete, without pretension or representation of life. I leave nothing here but breath and sensation—twilight breaking through the treetops, the fragrance of oak and ash leading down my nose. I shiver at the prospect of fire—what would be left in such a place after that? I see the magnificence of burning all around, as though it were more than a dream, but how might I dream so vaguely in passing with such violence and desire for destruction? Why, when the sunset is golden, is my sorrow thicker than these dead leaves floating down? I entertain reason by wondering how my sister*daughter* may have dropped herself in such a predicament. I know the full feeling of being a sibling. Of being an older sibling. Of being a sister*daughter*. In dark moments, I brought myself down with this awareness. I exist as myself, in power. Not over her, but in duty. Only I could help her in such a predicament, though I wonder why the boy felt himself unable to help her? Perhaps he saw her romantic hair sweeping across the peeling paint and feared some misunderstanding if he sought to untangle her from her confinement. Is that a halo in the sky? I ask myself and remember the blessings of former years...

My organs swell up with degradation. Between days and words, there was only the contemplation of myself, determined to break the accepted elements of life. I let her know none of this. She perceives very little, and we go about our lives in the sacred denial of my most heathen aspects. She is my sister*daughter*. There is no blasphemy that she could learn of that would not break that sacred bond. I anticipate this inevitability—suppress it. I'm tortured by it, but my imagination gets the better of me in such conditions. There was a vigilance to protect her at all costs, and yet here she is somewhere out beyond the forest, tied by her own most feminine aspect. I wander through the eerie wood as silent as a priest before his master. Hog, my flesh grows scarlet in the frozen air. I imagine a demon with a crown of hair, reaching up to the cosmos.

I step over coals as they burn and blossom as creatures of God and of Satan. I hear an evening bell toll at some great distance and feel the thrill of human life. The autumnal coldness does not break me. I am not dying. I know the green streams run by me. The silent houses sit on the edge of the world. There is my sister*daughter*, caught up in her predicament. Her soul lingers here and there, beside me. Is stronger than mine. Jagged flashes of light illuminate the trees, and I imagine her footsteps beside me here in the woods. Sick creatures weep, unsure of the darkness around us. I'm sure of the sounds, unsure of the dark silence in me that is so rare. When I feel the slow dripping—the blossoming of my dark heart—the solitary depths of womanhood here, would rise as angels. I have been rat, red sun, and black fly. My sister*daughter* will never know such things if I should say so. I would protect her from such petrified, frozen hours of life. I hear the music of strings, the wail of dark corpses. I would protect her from the banishment of her childhood at all costs if I could and drive myself mad in the making. The white knight screams on from the future. I am not yet in the nocturnal grip of the wood. Soft sounds bleed through, my steps grow older, the silence deepens. Black fir trees sway as though moved by giant hands. Blossoms of blue and white crumple underfoot. The dark autumn is tranquil. It is deceiving.

I stumble momentarily, wondering. I hear the rumble of mice, the cold steps of wolves. I touch a frozen finger to my mouth. My heart has always been a black globe, softly fading into nothingness, painted only with the frosting of sweet interactions with my young sister*daughter*. Drunk on wine and derelict imaginings, I find myself sheltering her from me—the skeleton of my former self. Enamored, enraptured, consumed by the approach death. What is it for a young girl to see someone rotting before her? When she has no one else to protect her? I would rear her up as though she were myself without pain, without memory, but she has horrors of her own, no doubt, even by that age. In the end she will be as dark as me, though tougher. This is the privilege of womanhood—to be so strong and so densely hidden within that there can be nothing but endurance. There is no pleasure in such a life, or very little of it. I think of her motionless and restricted in her condition. I think of the slowness of my passing through the woods, feel regret—feel the crumbling of my own dignity, and hurdle myself through the trees. I am exhausted in this old age dream, like scattering wind and leaves, like a monster. She need not my help. Who needs the help of a dark, broken thing?

The great green lamps and the tensions of the village. I return the memory of the woods. Sink deeper into myself, as does the melancholy of pushing further. I lose my patience with this charade. I feel like sobbing through the streets towards the house, imagining her small face close to mine. I am truly mad, am I not? Frightened of myself and this manner of touching and destroying, wishing for wellness, but doing only this. Who could ever think that life could be so inelegant? So demented? My soul undulates in excessive worry. I consider the possibility of possession—that I have lost my sensitivity in this tainted passage through life. The pain is unimaginable. I will not sleep. I will not eat. I will not read the fables and tales of old as I did. I have no patience for such things. There are labyrinths within me—layers of decay—the deepest being so strange, that I might think myself a demon walking on air in a cherry pink hat, in gold dressing, face obscured by rays of interminable color. I salute myself in this absurdity! For evil in absurdity cannot be so intolerable. I told myself such things in my boldest dreams, melting into spaces of retreat so that I could know myself as horrid, but not to be taken so seriously.

Lamps glow over the cobblestone streets. I am almost to the fence, breathing in the semi-darkness of the village, wondering when the first strand of ginger will shock my senses. My wrinkled lips part in the freezing air. I am—no doubt—sick now. Sicker than I was before the passage through the woods. These revelations of truth rush through my body, vandals of truth in a weakened shell. This phenomenal night has drawn me closer to death. I know not how or why passage through the natural—through wood and ice—could bring about such thoughts. Light evaporates overhead. The sun—once a skyless prison of branches—has become brighter, shielding me from the decay of life. I imagine my parents towering over me, the feeling of disappointment in them. I grow smaller and smaller, more diseased, contemplating the horror of myself, the limitless echo of their words gnashing against me.

I would raise her up so fiercely. There would be precious days of incoherence—experiments and indecorum. I imagine the highest spirits walking among her. Invisible sentinels circling, evaporating the darkness, lines of energy pulsing, only a method of approach that would bring her closer to this great problem—mortality.

The deep ache of my condition lingers. I am married to an inverted blessing. I cannot finish these contemplations. For a second, I dream of a wind that carries me up off of the ground and into the air, summoned by byrds. Emotions calls out, hideous and unmistakably human. I expect no less from my imagination. I am a shape on an edgeless globe. There is no feature so absolute that I cannot be wiped away by wind or light or fire or grain. I remember my father walking and groaning as he would pass by me, powerful and distressed. I became smaller and smaller, shrinking away into the nothingness of any room. So small that he could crush me with a single footstep.

I am incoherent. The wind rocks me. I am frozen, barefoot somehow—scrapes beneath my feet bleed. I imagine an empty winter coming towards me. I recognize the horror of life coming, coming. I flutter my eyelashes. I grimace. I tremble. I find her there because I want to find her there. Eyes settle upon something impossible. Immersed in the vulgarities of life, I wave on to an invisible water—a bodiless voice who knows me in the woods. I grew up in the darkness. The handle of my door remained locked, and I sat in fear of self-understanding. I have added another night to this contemplation of death. The sky bleeds into me, thoughts I cannot handle. I will be vigilant. I will sink into the white streaks of imagination, mist hanging over me. I swallow hard before the house, as I did in the wood.

I've come to the fence. She is not there. She is not anywhere. Sister*daughter* in my heart, so sacred that I might forget you were never there.

Will I ever have a sister?
daughter
        daughter
           daughter
daughter

daughterdaughter

CHAPTER SIXTEEN

THE PILLAR—AN obelisk—is composed of fragile teal particles, like salt from the sea of Ameeir. A seductive sight, I am absorbed into the gloom of the city square. Passersby ignore the structure. Embracing the silent hell of impatience, I stagger back, without expectation. There are things I must know and must learn, but without course or company, I blink at the silence of the evening. Unease flavors the dusk, as the city intends. Cursing quietly, an assault against myself, I almost miss the tendrils of black ink, painting the sky in words without meaning, without audience. A familiar spasm brings me to the ground. I remember mother most in moments such as these. Attentive and clear, ever-present, ever-near.

An inhuman bell tolls loudly from the tower down the fourth of nine streets. Children in colorless cloaks run—a stampede of anticipation—towards the fountain. They drop their garb against the cobblestones, crawling over the barrier and into the water. There are smiles and eyes swelling with sweetness, a momentary reprieve from the infinite tragic cosmos. I do not envy them their fun. Not entirely. Only mourn the absence of such experience, unsure if it was taken by the world outside or the world within.

Their features tell a tale of expectation. I watch in wonder as their skin turns to a faint shade of blue. A shade I recognize without hesitation. It is that of Von Aurovitch's blue lady.

This new dance would clear my head of the violent attention. I disrobe slowly, allowing myself a careful existence before the onslaught. A dark scent refreshes me. I am in everybody's eyes under the celestial stillness.

Feeling the warmth of my own frailty, I lose myself in shimmering light. A Sabbath of gloss and mistaken genius slides away.

Pink clouds weigh down my eyelids. At the zenith of self-reflection, I keep one hand on my stomach and one free. The panorama gives nothing but slime. Caught in a fright under dripping skies, I come to remember the sea as nothing, as everything, as magnificent and meaningless as myself. A shroud of velvet rustles in a distant corner. I dream the fool's dream of him being there.

Creatures of artifice, unhealthy bodies! I swell up in muteness. Eyes wander to the darker mysteries of the slime-sea gathering. I am reminded of my favorite tree—a willow, afflicted often by the suffocation of a cold breeze. Determined and calm, I know it is time to leave. The horizon is painted pink and gold. I forget the fluids of vanity and wallow in the rays.

The final version of myself will be a contradiction, caught in safe and deadly air.

I hold my hands still. The slime, the wetness—it is all familiar, but not so frightening as home. To which I speak, the passion of organs—there is more monstrosity there, in the limbs of men, than in the most primitive of beasts here. The horror lies in the illusion of evolution. That these things have evaporated from the forefront of thought as necessary, but as elements permissible of neglect. They are not.

A dance of light streams in every direction. At times, transparent sprouts pop out of my unkempt hair. Unordinary colors painted magic worlds. I awake on a white marble slab on a dizzy afternoon. Shaking my head, I find my tongue tangled with sweetness.

The horizon appears as fluff and brittle vapor.

I tiptoe over a pale stream of moisture. He is difficult, I think. I was unprepared. A scent of dust and cherries fell from the labyrinthine pink pools.

Desperation grips my soul, calmed only by skies of gray. My face bloats with attempts at cognitive diplomacy.

Damnable spirits roar from the blue swamp. The atmosphere keeps them quiet. Contained. But not without her thriving entirety, bursting through. The horrid history of the marsh doesn't lend itself towards light-hearted creatures. I have found Autura here, unshackled and alone. Not yet dispersed. I ask her why they have allowed her to live. She does not answer.

An ancient love fills her cup with white blood. The night sky opens, flickering violent rays and swallowing stars. A swarm of silence brings fatality to within arm's length. She waits in a madness of serpents. She calls out to the birds of earth, who hear slight pang of other worlds. A shiver or ache in the wing.

Why do I hold my heart against her? Why might she lower her head in thought? In spite of all, she faces me—her gold dress flowering, blooming, crossing in front of her in the dark. The light lifts from the horizon. My head splits. My cynicism blossoms to a point of sharpness so intense that a white flare scares my thoughts. I am clumsier than she. Darker. There is too much ambition inside of me, and I wonder how I might be free from such a thing in this body. My mind rises. Convulsions rock my limbs. I remember her undulations—the softness of her movement. *Count on me, darling girl,* she says.

The world is ruled by sleep. I swallow pink drops—the powder of the skies. There is grace in her speech. She reaches out and pulls my hair away from my face. I am not as pale as she. My lips are not as full. My cheekbones not as high. My heart not as white. I detach myself from this madness, fearing that I might harm her more that I should. That she may suffer as freely as I had alone in the woods. Where did she come from? Where has she truly been before all of this? I try to embrace the calm that is looking into a face that knows the universe—that knows me. We are surrounded by flowers and traveling light. She speaks and I listen attentively, concentrating on her mouth—on the sound of her voice. Her generosity. Her intelligence. My reactions are slow and contained.

She is as I may have been, had I not been ill. Had I not been broken. Had I not been touched by the darkness of love. But in this, I fool myself. She has met with the same heart, the same body. He appeared in her vicinity as festive and as empty as in mine. Her forehead flushes with fever, and I know that she has been touched by the yellow illness of the Afterworld. She will sink into the flat earth, beneath serpents, beneath blood, beneath the gray fabric of this doom.

What do they want of her? Clouds move in over the garden. Her body rocks forward and backward. Her silence cuts open the sky, cloud trails of black and white gold flowers sprouting up. *They think I will bring them the new slime.* My blindness is boundless. I answer, not wanting to admit to myself the bond between us. I will choke back these regrets. There is enough hurt in her and helplessness in me to preserve the moment of grace. They want to pull me through the black forest, she says—the wood so unlike the others. One hundred dreams of hard work cannot match the menace of those woods. I remember my ancestry. She reminds me of her. I remember mother, dark galaxies of thought within her hair.

What will you do, I ask her, in dread of a danse macabre—a last display of beauty before death.

I will tear out this tired resentment within me. Retrieve my soul from the torment of the stone room—a place in my heart of scarlet injury. Music sounds only in memory of love and dark ecstasy. I will save myself and know myself as you see me.

In your green eyes of glass, what will become of me? I ask her, buried in the sparkle of dawn.

A child grows within you, Anonyma.

CHAPTER SEVENTEEN

THERE IS NOTHING to fear. The fathoms of mortality stretch on to a black infinity.

I do not enter the labyrinth but am made aware of the arch before it. Staggering dizzily, I fall and stand and fall again. Dawn will fade the terror of this place. I will stand again.

What is woman without a name? A tool, a treason, a tyrant? A figment of the imagination? Without worth, or saved from recompense? What is a woman without birth? Am I empty? Am I empty? Dead cities of unread letters, all inside these drawers. Not a single one from him, but several from his betters.

Don't these people tire of dead rooms? Spaces without life, or need to breathe? I will waste no such time here. I am the Star assembled on the faerie's battlefield. Graced by magic dust on a globe of blue. I am the wisp of wonder in the highest hall called to duty in a course-less dream. I would be awake in such a way if captivity gave way to a heightened scream. Yesterday I was fragile. Today, only pale. In times my hands pass over my breasts, I feel the most alive. Some nights I run my hands over my body in such a way that I almost cannot tell that they are mine.

I am not a victim at this age. Only a sea of memories tied up in graying bows. The ripeness has gone from me, as I knew it would. I age older than even myself in backwards minutes and broken hours. Everything slides back to me as I realize time has made its peace. *You are so young*, they say. But I know better.

I imagine dead vines snaking through me, atop the rot. Debris strewn over, like life in excerpts. The photos ripped and bloody, like the inside. Veins without color, beyond the sight of man, connect me to the stars above. I am horribly uprooted, though only for a time.

The silence shines like rubies in a grave of the undead. I stretch my poisons out on a sailor's earth. I remember taking scissors to the fringe in the darkness of my bedroom. He will not know me now, in this condition. Not as he has made me. I want, with all my heart, to believe that I have overcome time. But this relies on an assumption of terms with which time will not agree. Might I be pureness in this instant, even without a name?

Old passion survives within him, but it is a worm's passion. Always burrowing in deeper dirt, if only to seek shelter from the sun.

What about Autura, who did good and lived as one should? She obeyed and did what she did not desire, and so met with the lesser evil in the material world. What of it? Might I not feel guilt for not acting the same?

I am compelled to follow, but refrain. Here is my divinity, what men will see as weakness. When I walk on air, it will be, to them, as though it never occurred.

Cruelty flourishes under the red wrath—the will of Angel-Lord Menchen. The ghosts, diminished in his vision as a madness of serpents, continue beyond the rocky outcrop of the Meadow of Ornament, towards the black woods.

Exposed to admiration for the first time, I beg to be released from the commitment. I shoulder my own absence with distress. My downfall is self-described, self-designed, self-fulfilled. But what may have become of me in a different light?

I deny the reality of a fragile body, she says. And in this denial, lurks condemnation. That I, as I am—feeble, wavering—continue only as invalid. So why should I exist on earth, a living thing? I don't like to think that we have to earn consciousness, but that we have to earn a body—or to keep one—is another matter. I cannot dance as she does. Not in this body. Not in this life.

The vessel is a mess, of this there is no doubt. I writhe in the decrepitude of the organic shell, unsure of how it can be alive in the moment, given history. Given time.

A crystal voice bleeds through this worry. The beating of nocturnal wings are heavy overhead. I am a glorious multitude, glowing from the center, out into the limitless night. I am seen by things unknown, heard in places unreachable. To these strangers of the cosmic deep, I have a name.

There are no sights to see beyond the hideous flapping. My spirit droops, lamenting God and the loss of all things human. The city glows in the distance, scarlet carved in glass. Each step on thorn and acid aches from foot to forehead.

If angels should beckon to these lustful moors, I imagine them to be pillars of salt—timeless and unfeeling.

I walk the streets in solitude, and know I am not alone. The echoes call to me from the distant rain. Quiet plants graze my arms by the stream, as I walk by with a book in hand. The ground shakes—subterranean elements shrieking out as icy phantoms, wisps of light, curling around the fingers and evaporating.

Worth begins with the first earth-breath, I imagine. In a sea of faith, I will become a different person. Tattered black cloth coaxed my lungs to breathe. I hand the marble heart of envy to this man of stone. I forfeit this flesh to the bodiless world.

I stumble on a ripe pear, half-sunken in the dead earth. The city, as forgotten as death, senses my coming departure—like the snowbird on a ballad of Spring.

The vastness of unimaginable worlds grows deeper. Panic-stricken, crowds gather in the street, summoned by gentle, anguished cries.

A star, burned out, galloping in embers over each abyss, knows no dimension as home—no place as final. Seeking a strange arrangement without breath, a human sound becomes a howl of weakness. I let this pain pass as a certain awareness.

CHAPTER EIGHTEEN

THE WIND SMELLS of rot and forced violence. I imagine the formless walls of the Afterworld. The Meadow of Ornament, the Bridge of Sighs. Sadness looms larger than him, Nicholas, directing his malice towards me for this failure. It is his, not mine.

The procession has arrived, doused in stellar dust from the open ceiling. They pour on me blessings of despair. I wander through the water of time and feel doubt. Women weeping, their hearts held against the moon, their opacious breasts bare against the wind. Spirit shoulders held against the Temple, consuming both name and universe. I shudder as blood pours from invisible clouds. The silver mountain, unperverted and unyielding, cloth'd in the holiness of singed feathers. The Doom Artists—they are to devour the multitudes, but only after supper. The desert stretches on, deadly in sleep. Gray voices sing fragile tones of terror.

The procession stops in the city square. I consider a fear, as yet unborn: that there is more to the despair of this evening than I can anticipate. The great coffin shivers and breaks open. Inside lies Autura—copper hair arranged around her in delicate waves, her body covered in sheer lavender linen, with little contrast against her ashen skin.

Her exhaustion ends in this air of madness. Autura awakens, dispelling memories into the mist like air, she sees the reflection of herself in dim light. Surrounded by bronze paint and mud, nudity and filth, confusion and guilt.

Bound, bloody, encircled by familiar figures. Envy held her heart against the world, though the distant wetness of her forgotten life made her alert. A solemn desperation grips her, dripping with the divine goodness of her former youth and the heavy atrophy of each paralyzed year.

She sits up, seeing the ring of coffins around her. Sisters in dust. A great horn rings out from the dark horizon. She stands, seeing me, seeing herself. Her arms rise up, a ritual, reaching to the firmament.

Only in this silence would I see her power. With a beggar's knowledge of the great ominous dusk, Autura steps out of her coffin. She bears her breasts in the shower of dust and weeps gently. So bleak, is this world without giving. So strange is this sky without light. I have deep feelings about my own broken body—about its possibilities, but none as great as this. Here I am half-awake, unsure of her—unsure of myself. A cloud of red sand rises in the distance.

They are coming.

She draws a half-moon in the dirt with her left foot, pressing her shoulders against the wind, rolling them back gracefully. Her fingers lengthen, bent with folkloric strength. Autura's arms roll up and down sensually, framing her body, combinations of unearthly movement flowing through her without thought or strain. Her rib cage slides from left to right, stomach undulating, rolling. She drops her right hip down, without moving her upper body. Her pelvis tucks in and releases out, feet stomping on the ground, shaking the air, shaking us.

Autura glides across the earth, alive and magnificent, transferring her weight from one leg to the other to an unheard rhythm. Our sisters emerge from their coffins, pale, but living. Hammering, cooing, clawing has reduced them to wisps of their earthly selves. Pain coiled into a strange outer magic. Doom Design, I fear. The muffled beating of madness from the outer lands. Hips roll clockwise one two three four hair thrown upward nine steps to the south and four to the west on and on. The black cloud slides closer, creeping towards the city square. Punctuated by the sighs of marveling spectators, I see in her eyes what has never been there before. Pure pleasure. The previous wind, crisp and agitating, grows warm. She struggles and falls to her knees, head upright, hair streaming over her, glowing.

Radiance gleams from the pillar. A strange, amethystine vapor sweeps out from the base of the columns, growing taller, wrapping itself around the coffins.

Growing faint, the women slump onto the ground, losing their color again.

The black cloud invades the square. Lightning crackles down, striking the pillar. It shatters in slow-motion. The corpses respond to the gentle notion, a slower dance. Inclined to bend her wrist, it swirls towards me as she stands again. Autura slides her foot a few inches back, pressing it against the cobblestones. Shifting her weight down, her hair sweeps from left to right, a pendulum of strands, as seductive as the convergence of pink and black sky overhead. Ancient Uldreds fly over—gnarled limbs like dug-up tree roots, baleen teeth snarling, an ancient grimace. Only the unnatural could invert beauty so precisely. She recoils close to the ground as the hands of Uldred fliers reach down into the crowd. Dragged through gold dust, beams of white mist grow dim. The surrounding miles, exposed to this event, regain their color in waves.

At last, ultimate possibility had fallen to bitterness and resignation. How grandiose is loyalty in the vast space of nothingness. A single lamp lights the soul in pieces, suggesting a fading moon over seas of slime. There is a great confusion sinking into the square at the dissolution of the dance. The spectators grow lethargic. Spirits take flight as the miracle of warmth dissolves into ice-without-color.

Autura does not weep. She does not despair. She is shackled to her splintered coffin again, fragments scraping her naked body into a pulp. It floats above the rest, shutters, and follows the procession of Uldreds back towards the hopeless necropolis.

The people flee in panic as a red glow carries down from the north. My stomach is heavy with expectation. Green foam pours from the other coffins. The women disintegrate, a mess of yellow flesh and white dust. In this dance, she says to me, I lift my sisters up, because I have known death in the arms of men.

CHAPTER NINETEEN

THERE WAS A time I found myself angry and magnificent. I smashed the ground under heel with the mass of my own torment. Inviting fury to my door—to chew, to spit, to maim—the repugnance of my body praised as deadly, magic vapor.

I remember the rolls of the belly, the pulsing of the heel. The twists and turns and pleasure of Raqs Sharqi—the dance of my sisters.

Black birds spiral over the city. Uldred hands grasp my weakened elbows. The great courthouse awaits, as does the deranged Doom Artist.

Swarms of ghouls stare aslant—those I know and have never known. I remember the black celestial writings scribbled in a monstrous hand. Bells ring there from the unknowing distance. Bodies and spirits float past my face, like milk in the slipstreams of shattered glass. All eyes watch the great seat. Doors shut and we are in the inescapable frame of injustice—the place of decision in the Afterworld.

There are those who would take to 2,000 years of wandering after leaving this place just to quell the horror.

Eyes of palest yellow roll backwards. Accosted by eternal damnation—this is the disease we know to have swept through these lands. Clearly visible on the pulpit is Autura—face badly bruised, standing erect despite the shivering—despite pain. She has not been out stripped of her glory. Even the hearts of those strange things that look weak and sneer and laugh know her to be a magnificent thing. They see nothing in me. Not yet. There is a slice of life in me, resigned to the point of power known only in those who have met with violence on earth. Under a resplendent ceiling with crackles and demonic ornament, the great thing sweeps down from the summit—its flight leading towards the great chair of judgement. Constellations twinkle through my mind those strung up and waiting have not been broken by what they have witnessed. They live, though as shadows—as caverns—as living and as dying as anything.

I would not injure her again. She lives and breathes of me, and so I hide my face behind a black sheath. Will she not know me by the lantern? Its gold and ornament twinkly under? Its cobalt hut? The Doom Artist, enormous wings folding up towards the great chair of judgement, lets out a deep, growling sigh. The air is cold now. Devastating wind escapes the chamber. Swooping down to this gothic vault of doom—of dereliction—I feel the immensity of death. Its grip upon me, pain, sorrow—all. There are many things in waiting here. Many limbs. Barren, fantastic, bleak, and black wardrobe is found in waves through swaying lamplight. Unknown colors illustrate the audience. There is a festivity to this vast injustice. Swarms of black flies glitter and go up to the heights of the chamber—tunneling, circling, streaming materials forming the mass of my anxiety, reaching up into the absolute—into everything.

Much was promised to her. Secret gestures, gentle kisses, the passion of black and white. This is an old city. I know this now. I have felt the vulgarity in the pretension. I have seen the grotesque façades of the broken buildings. Streets of dirt, shattered glass panes, splintered wood painted with blood and webs. I have known the suffering of lit interiors. Of the former world. Of little girls and women. Where everywhere was darkness lit by red and gold. I motion towards the floor in anguish. I catch myself in the immensity of despair. There are oceans of suffering within her, as there are within me. I breathe out, and I believe she sees this.

We are now in the hour of decline. I see the silver drops fall from her eyes. They are not of sadness but of completion. The remnants of ancient royalty. A blackbird sweeps down from the great opening in the ceiling—strange beast of melancholy. There is a mild silence before the twisting ghoul at her feet yells,

Her womb is barren.

My eyes fall upon the strangest of the onlookers, a deathly-white man, as human as any I had seen, a bundle of orange curls in a regal updo. His garb had all the pomp and ornament as the richest of men.

"Remember this, young Doom Artist," a ghoul whispers to me.

I cannot understand the Uldreds. Only an occasional word will sing into me, calling up a recollection from the *Scaearulldytheraeum*. She answers,

"I dress myself in my own horror so you may not dress me in it, undress me in it, address me in it. It is entirely mine and mine to wield."

They cut her deeply, and I feel it. Her blood is my blood. Her sounds are my sounds. Overcome by fullness, a deep pulsing between heart and stomach, I lurch forward. All attention is gone from the limbless corpse before them—Autura in the folds of death, breath caught in the streams of whispers above, transporting her to another air, another snow. They split her open. There is nothing in her womb. They have all turned to me, removing their masks to reveal faces eaten by worms.

I am on my knees, in the agony of love. My daughter lives within me. I hear her, as distinctly as death fills the chamber with the haunt of nothing. Feel her move and squirm, aching to come out, to live. I am here in this aggression before change. The first day of logic after long leanings in the dark. I know that I must leave this place. So little time is left. So little reason to feel as I feel. I fall into a deep slumber. Born and bred a fiendish dreamer, I wheeze and cry at the madness of a blank slate of dreams. Black light, withering sound.

Glancing into the night sky—anxiety-ridden, nervous—I withdraw from the air of the unnatural world. A small moment. I keep it for myself, without a word.

Circling the path in black soot, closing in on the idea of nothing, I remember myself progressive and unafraid, in the air, in the sea, among the living. Gestures swell from body to mind, a release of gold into the great reaches of the sky. I forgive myself in the scene—

without exaggeration. The crowd pours out into the street. Struck by the fever of black noise, the onslaught of memory, I fall back, into heart-seclusion. I hear my name. My voice, and another, a pitch etched with hunger and love.

There is no wisdom in the panic of these streets. There is a bird of bright yellow far above me, yet still far behind. My golden mouth remembers old wounds. I vanish from the crowd, swelling with smoke. Hummingbirds swoop, blood pours, bubbles froth and fall from mouth to stone. I run until the sea of slime is before me. I steal death from the eyes of angels when I plunge into the depths as myself. Blood swims in the venom of my voice. Far from here, glory echoes, for me to reach in my own time.

I awaken in a room without life. Crystals dangle over me from the old chandelier. Curtains sway the delicate motions of the night winds. He is here.

"You have come back to me," he chokes out. My eyes remain on the ceiling. "Soon you will dance as you once did."

CHAPTER TWENTY

THE STAGE IS miraculous. Woven in snow, the wonderment of the dark Thuringian wood, as he had always described it. Songs of dead eternity leap through my body. The hallucination lives beneath my skirts.

Fresh snow sweeps down, grazing a body in the heat of fright. The vaulted ceiling shines down in quiet rays—chipped gold onto gentle white hands, held precious, and in pain. A light flashes in his eyes—morbid gusts of memory—love, loss, a terrible fight to shut down the coming awareness of all that is to be.

I limp on stage, in a white dress. The landscape of blue light and snow is disorienting. I know this place, and collapse to my knees.

The audience is in awe of me. To them it is incredibly moving and pure.

Nicholas kneels down, lifting my face him.

Do you remember?

His voice is different from the other performance. It has a menacing, abhorrent cadence. A strange sound comes from overhead onstage. Metal shifting on a rig. I look up to see the shadow of the icicle. It is being moved into place. I know that it is no theatrical prop. It is a means an end.

My love is in league with a hell of missing names, calling all demons in for dark collection. Had I not bowed my head to that old death desire, letting limb and liquid fall down on his floor, I may not have come to this place. That evil, a surface-wish, could never reach the deepest realm of myself, stirring up that which hides, which festers, allowing such pain to rise up to the skin. His ashes stain my lips, and a fatigue of emptiness consumes me. It never will, again.

The sound of the rope and metal rig sounds. I pull away from him. He struggles to keep me in place. The jagged icicle descends from the heights of the trees and impales him from behind. The tip of the icicle is inches from my face, an ejaculation of blood and flesh soaking me. A ritual of death-in-life.

The audience is silent, watching me, watching them.

Caked in the aftermath of dark love, my eyes maintain a cosmic blur. Colors wavering, shapes indescribable. I feel my mother's arms lift me up, as they did so long before this. She is carrying me. Carrying me away. I'm on the floor of the living room. Mother is washing away the blood from me. I close my eyes and feel the grit of damp rags rage against my skin.

I am reborn in myself a storm, facing outward.

To everything that was wondrous and stark, feeble and fantastic, I hold a candle. Staring at a sliver of a moon through crooked glasses, cracking lanky fingers over broken sills. Broken, blessed, forgotten, remembered. Entirely myself.

A machine of enchantment, he emerged from the shadows, the personification of supernatural mesmerism, as cruel as any orchestrated evil had ever been on the earth. Might I accompany him on this path of cold greatness? No. There are streams of memory that allow for such mistakes, but even I know of the deliberate within me. There is no thirst for death any longer.

My delicacy is no fault of my own, but of the universe, and the age of unreason. There are sensibilities that shall remain curious in the age of science, dismissed for lack of logic or measurement. I am the embodiment of such curious tools of the unnatural. Nicholas knew this, sought it out, marveled at its manifestation in me. I know that I am nothing to him without this gift, this power that is no power at all. He cannot know what I know—that magic, whatever that is or may become, is not something to wield over others, over oneself. It is only something visited upon a body, a mind, a heart, in vulnerable moments, in fragility, and gone as suddenly, without evidence.

In days of brazen ego, I thought myself the greater darkness, and likened myself to the worst of all among them. I see the desperation in that now. To feign a harsher skin among monsters.

Each, now, I find are bones beneath unmarked graves. Many a longtime admirer pitched in to pay for his lovely stone. As they stand in life, so they do in death.

There is no nostalgia in this—seeing a beast among men, interred. Only something of a passing grace for me. Where others may beg of me to spit and pass over this monument – I sit and say a silent thank you to things I cannot know.

EPILOGUE

IN A REFLECTION in a mirror, I see my life play out again. A single drop – soon to evaporate in the rising of this new and gentle morning, slides down against the gold frame.

Washed away in years of quiet fading are the leaves of trees untamed in those times of horror. I think upon them slowly now, with gentle touches to the chest with wrinkled hands. These hands—living and dead—the skin flaking off, as my soul flakes from this earth. The time has come now to put away these recollections. I will pick them up again when I have had time for rest. There is no dream of fancy that awaits me on this night.

Thick, dark curls and a wide face, like mom's. The icy blue eyes. Her father's. My lips, full lips. And an almost indescribable shade of skin. Dark, with spectral undertones suggesting a touch of magic in the blood. She is my daughter. I hold her face in my hands and feel a celestial unity. Marvelous universe. Miraculous life! I hold her, here—close to my chest—where the dark cast of the ages cannot find her.

Someday I will know this separation. Will face it with the agony of a golden limb being torn from me without numbness. Her glory will live in that moment, far from me, becoming herself, blossoming in a world fit to destroy us, all for being woman and unquiet.

With strength unusual for her age, she splashes water, laughter gleaming out of her as moonbeams, my face dripping with the remnants of her playtime.

I hum softly, carrying her out of the water. Holding her. She breathes the warmth of peace, of love. She is mine and I am hers and that is all of the universe I need to know.

ABOUT THE AUTHOR

Farah Rose Smith was born and raised in Rhode Island. Her writing has appeared in *Lackington's Magazine, Darker Magazine (Russia), Spectral Realms, Vastarien: A Literary Journal, Nightscript, Dead Reckonings*, and more. Smith holds a BA in Comparative Literature from Hunter College and is currently working towards a master's degree in English Literature, Language, and Theory, focusing on Disability Theory, Medieval Studies, Supernatural Fiction, Decadence, and the Russian Silver Age. She lives in New York City with her husband and their three cats.

GRIMSCRIBE PRESS